# The Atheist Bible

## Michael Leamy

*To Randy Herman,*

*I suspect you understand* :)

Copyright © 2012 Michael Leamy
All rights reserved.
ISBN:978-0-9921584-4-6

All characters appearing in this work are fictitious.
Any resemblance to real persons, living or dead, is purely coincidental.

Layout and Cover Design by CopperSpoon Publishing.
Editing by Veronica Knox of Silent K Publishing.

Also available in digital format
ISBN: 978-0-9921584-0-8 (ePub)
ISBN: 978-0-9921584-1-5 (Kindle)

For mom.

She taught me to ask "where's the beauty?"

# ACKNOWLEDGMENTS

Like so many seemingly small things, a great many people have helped make this work possible. These are the people I want to send my appreciation to.

My wife, Shauna Leamy, and my three kids Kelsey, Kieran and Erin. When the world was telling me to stop they gave me the encouragement and support I needed to keep working. There is nothing as motivating as your children asking about 'the book.'

Veronica Knox, my editor, put in more hours than I care to admit. While I worked to make sure my symbolic elements made sense, her guidance ensured the most grievous of my grammatical and continuity errors didn't interrupt their hidden dialogue.

... and Mark Jackson, for the letter 'F.'

## JULY 5     1

> "Forgiveness is not a unique or absolute product of the religious mind."

I've come to see this as my first atheist thought. That's important, because I think it killed my wife.

The sun is coming up, and I've been awake for two days. There is a park outside my hospital window, a wide rolling field dotted with oaks and maples, and even with my limited vision it is very pastoral in this summer weather. I can also see a large branch, its bark thick from age, swinging gently in the breeze. The tree itself is out of my line of sight, but it must be very close to the building as the foliage is nearly touching the glass. Its leaves are a vivid, living green, and they accent the more sombre and earthy greens of the grass beyond. If what the doctors tell me is true, I'll be here long enough to watch those leaves change. Fall will come, and on such majestic old trees as these, the colours will probably be spectacular. I'm not in too much pain right now, as long as I don't move. I suppose that isn't a big surprise considering the amount of drugs they've been feeding me, and that's nice. To be able to disconnect from the pain and just heal.

They tell me the car was totalled. They tell me I'm lucky to be alive.

Four ribs shattered. Both legs and my right arm in traction, with my hand looking like a science experiment. My jaw is wired shut, and my face feels swollen and hot. I'm guessing the bandages on my head do nothing to hide the fact I probably look like a ghoul. The list goes on. Internal bleeding, and a line of stitches along my hip that will leave a truly manly scar. I was told they removed an impressive collection of junk from a hole punched into me just above my pelvis, and when I asked what it was, they said it appeared to be the contents of the glove box.

The glove box. In my guts.

I try to lean over, I want to see if my one good arm can reach the water, and a searing pain tears up my spine. Of course the cup is just beyond my reach on the day table. I'm guessing the wheels are really slick, because I've noticed it moves all over the room as the day wears on. From the moment I woke up yesterday I haven't been able to reach it. They've pinned the call button to my sheets near my good hand, and after some fumbling, I trigger it to see if I can summon a nurse or an aide to help me get a drink. For the briefest moment I dream, allowing my head to wander back in time. Just a moment.

She did it on purpose. I'm broken and she did it on purpose.

The bright red light blinks reassuringly above my head to let me know the call button has been activated, and I lay unwillingly on my back, thinking bedsore thoughts, as I begin the wait. I am now officially meat, and I have been since I arrived. A warm sack of formerly human goo that makes noises and leaks at various times of the day and night.

The management of the leaks, the wrappings, the weights and the pillows - that's the job of the hospital. I won't be human again until some time after I leave this place, this horrible, terrible place I need so much, which they assure me will actually happen. Until then I am maintained and managed.

As time passes, the call light remains busy just beyond my sight. I know this from its reflection on the thirty-year-old traction rig, the tubes alternating from industrial grey to industrial pink, and my mind sinks deeper into this dreamy blank state. I'm floating and waiting. The drugs in my heart making my love for myself personal. I watch the light tinker with the clock, and it just keeps flashing, steady and perfect, while I imagine watching the nurses ferry syringes to and fro. Back and forth. Fill the syringe and empty the syringe. Rush to the desk and fill out a form, while the light beckons to them from the console.

I am room 4b. I know my light is blinking at them over drugs and pens, while papers witness the time passing and I'm still afloat in my room, anxious and waiting to get a drink from my wandering table. I've been awake for two days, and the routine of being a passive patient has asserted itself so strongly, I don't even think to question it. I am pliant. I do as I'm told. I wait for what I need, and if I'm lucky they will bring me drugs. I'm not in too much pain, as long as I don't move, but yesterday when I first woke up, I was. Great pain. It was so large and so vast, I wanted to use colours to describe it. Nothing mattered to me but the pain, and as I think these thoughts my little red light keeps distracting me, insisting I watch its repetitive boredom on the traction bars over my head. With a jarring suddenness it occurs to me the pain will return, in fact I can feel it trying, and my call light becomes a bit more important. I'm thirsty, and as I look at my sterile room, I hope they remember to give me my pain meds as well. My drugs. Mine, and I want them to know it. I want a drink, and I'm in pain, and I'm becoming afraid.

What has she done to me?

*"Nothing you didn't ask for ... nothing you didn't deserve."*

I loved her. What the hell am I supposed to do now?

I'm going back again. Time is contracting and I'm trying not to see. The green walls are bare, save for the tubes and connectors and lights all hospital rooms seem to need, and I'm trying not to think how I ended up in this bed, afraid of a pain I can feel creeping towards me from the shadows, unable to remember a time when I was brave.

I think I killed my wife, and for my trouble she tried to kill me back.

*"You did not kill me, you saved me, and I tried to save you."*

I really need to get out of this hospital. I'm not going to survive it. The drugs are keeping me alive, but they feel like they're killing me to do it.

I've been awake for two days, and I don't want to remember my life. I wish I could fall back into my bed, to float and not care, but the light hurts my head, and I'm feeling time pass more urgently. It's like I've just walked into a room, interrupting a fist fight. The vibrating tension in the air is shaking my broken bones and I don't understand why. I wish the light would stop. I wish my wife had not tried to kill me. I wish I could find my time. I can't feel my feet, and my legs look too large.

The sun is shining through the window, and the trees in the park remain bright and beautiful. Persistently normal. I can feel the panic rising, and I try to listen to the outdoors. Something from reality that can help me stay sane. These rough hospital blankets are smothering me, and I strain to hear through the window. Glass lets in the light, but I need a sound, any sound. On the branch I can see a small yellow bird. I want to hear it sing. I look closer and I can see its small beak move, but no sound accompanies the motion. Focus on the bird, I tell myself, watch it sway on the branch and watch the beak. The motion of sound. The look of sound. I know it exists, because I've heard it before.

With effort, I find I can hear him singing.

The faint song isn't able to easily penetrate this room's convalescent fog, but I've brought as much of it in as I can, and I won't let go. The light keeps its anxious time over my head and I hear a bird on a branch outside my window. He's chirping. The bird is a Yellow Warbler. Dendroica Petechia. A male. I don't know how I know this, but I trust the knowledge and refer to him as he in my mind. I have him in my head, holding onto the real world by seeing him speak. The hint of the sound is keeping the call light away from me. I can't see it anymore and suddenly I'm a bit safer.

I feel a small bravery trying to return to me, and the joy of its arrival makes me larger. I take a slightly deeper breath.

A gun goes off in my chest and I stop everything. My heart. My lungs. My blood and my bile. I stop it all to allow my body to live through the pain my deep breath has somehow triggered. The bird is gone. My courage is gone. I'm once again cowering and alone, and the jarring red curse, endlessly counting the seconds over my head, is going to make me scream.

> *"This is your reward. Your atonement. Your lack of faith has angered God and you are being punished!"*

"Enough! Stop!" I yell at her through the grotesque remains of my lips, but the pain and the wires reduce my effort to choked whispers.

"Nurse!" I try to yell. A croaking wad of steaming meat makes a splashing noise.

There is no God. There are no gods. I cry to the walls and the blankets, silently screaming my pain into the universe as I tell my bird companion the gods are not real, and it will need to deal with its bird life alone, and I'm crying because knowing doesn't make the pain go away.

The nurse walks in to find me quietly sobbing. In between sobs I'm muttering incoherently to myself, at least to her, and she reaches over my trapped body and turns off the call light. A part of me senses its absence, but I can't stop feeling my heart beating, caged in my chest. She glances at her watch and makes a note in my chart while I gurgle next to her. I open my eyes a bit wider and see she is lifting my blanket, probably to check my bandages. I can see her face, that passive face of the common action, and I watch as it changes in front of me. She sees what I see, I know it. She sees there are no gods to save us anymore, and she feels her own panic rising. It's right there in her eyes. My blanket falls from her hand and I feel better knowing I'm not alone. I can feel my body floating in the bed, a soft cotton sphere. She reaches for me and we console ourselves in the warmth, a wash of love coursing through me. I love everything. I don't care about the past anymore.

I killed my wife, and for that she tried to kill me and now she's dead. My wife is dead, and I am in love with the universe in the arms of my nurse, as I bleed through my bandages and into my slowly filling lungs.

# JULY 7 — 2

My home. I have a home.

The night is quiet on the ward and my hearing is improving. The curtains are drawn on my window in the evenings because the lights illuminating the parking lot make it hard for patients to sleep. Without the view, I find the time passes more quickly thinking. Laying in bed with my wide thoughts keeping me company, and during this selfish time it just now occurs to me, I have a home, a home full of life, and I'm not there to take care of it.

It's an old two story brownstone full of plants, two large tanks of the fish and corals I've been nurturing for years, and a young cat I've been sharing dependency issues with. The cat's name is Franklin, and I named him that for no better reason than it popped into my head looking at him for the first time. He's an especially beautiful animal, at least I think so, with shortish hair that's nearly perfectly black. Franklin has always been healthy, but I've been here for about seven days, and he can't get out to forage for food while I'm gone.

"Franklin will starve ... help him ..." The sound of my broken voice grates my ears, and the words are unrecognizable. My soul feels stained.

I think of my fish in their large saltwater tanks. Marine tanks. Hard to maintain, and not something any random person can walk into the house and check. Salt levels, protein levels, light levels, heat levels, acid levels, every level has to be perfect or the minute ecosystem of the tank dies. The fish die. The corals die. Even the damn rocks die if I'm not watching everything like a hawk. It's been seven days, and I suspect even with professional help I might have already lost them - and then I remember that until now I hadn't even given them a thought.

I feel like I've betrayed them. Franklin and my nameless fish.

Franklin is not a large cat, but I haven't left any food out I can remember, so I know he is suffering. The thought crushes me, and in my head I see myself getting up, and with courage beyond my species, I make my way home. He sees me crawling up the cold stone steps, with bandages trailing behind me and blood in my eyes, and his look of appreciation is there, right there in the window, and I see it. We have connected, and we share the feeling of joy together, because I've saved him from certain death, and he loves me for it.

A patient cries in the room next to me and I realize I'm dreaming.

Five days of torture. They tell me my body is healing, and I'm being dragged along for the wretched ride in spite of myself, but I know my mind is toppled. I don't trust my eyes or my heart. I can't stop my mental wandering. One minute I hope the pain meds are coming, and the next I try to forget what Hellen looks like.

Hellen is my wife.

My wife tried to kill me.

Hellen tried to kill me.

Now she won't leave me alone.

It's too much, way too much emotion and I start to sob again. After the incident two days ago, every movement is dangerous - they still haven't figured out what collapsed my right lung and caused me to tear my stitches. They will soon; they've assured me they have been working on arranging the operating theatre and the proper specialists to make it happen, but until then I have to keep as still as possible so I don't start the bleeding again.

I wake up short of breath, and they drain the fluid out of my lung with a tube.

The sobs will go away soon, as they have before, and the fear I feel in the darkest part of my consciousness is helping put them down. Hellen is the topic I can't touch. She's the golden dagger, and my still-beating heart her sacrificial target. I just hope I'm not insane.

The walls are dark and the ward is quiet. The patient in the room next to me was electrocuted while moving a stove in his home, and the electricity blew off a part of his leg. The cries I hear from him coincide with my own constrained agonies, as we both weep, inside and out, for the coming of the pain killers. Our lives are being lived in four-hour increments, and the woozy sleep of narcotic lust is what we are each trying to achieve. His cry a few minutes ago makes me wonder if we are due, but I'm not feeling much discomfort, and I wonder if perhaps there is something other than physical suffering making him yell.

I am alone in my room and the past is making me cry, making me feel I've lost what little mind I have left. Perhaps my neighbour is alone as well, and if there are demons who feed on our singular visions in time, could they be at him too?

*"We are all God's children, and we will all be saved."*

Hearing her voice, I feel my body attempt to run a chill down my spine, but the damaged parts of me are holding so tightly to control, the chill is stifled. I can feel my jaw is trying to hold the tension in spite of the pain it's bringing to me, and although I can't tell, I fully expect I'm grinding my teeth. How much does it take to chip a tooth with your jaw wired shut? Will it hurt?

The lives in my charge take back my thoughts, and I remember I'm facing a problem.

How am I going to get help for my cat and my fish, when I can't even speak?

I reach up slowly with my good arm and try to grab hold of the nurse's chart. It is sitting on the edge of that fucking rolling table, and if I can just get hold of it perhaps I can write something down. The effort is more painful than I expected though, and although I can get my hand up to the chart, I don't have the strength to grasp it. The drugs and the damage have made me so weak I can't even hold the pen, so I slowly lift and drop my blunted arm in an effort to move the chart closer. I imagine an observer would see my efforts as feeble, but to me I'm a superhero. I keep lifting my arm, the pain in my side burning away my reason and logic, and the hand I know belongs to me keeps opening. My fingers rest softly on the board, and each time they make the trip I cheer inside, but it's a sham. They are simply resting against the papers. Resting against the thin aluminum of the clipboard. When I try to pull them down my fingers slide off, leaving no trace. My skin is as dry as the papers I've been trying to move, and they aren't able to generate enough friction to tease my goal anywhere nearer to me.

My mind cracks slightly as I repeat this futile dance.

I'm so weak. How can I live like this? I'm trapped in this broken shell while my whole world slowly dies. I don't want to hurt them. I don't want to return home to an abattoir of my failures. Franklin has done nothing wrong, so why does my injury have to hurt him?

My wife tried to kill me, and instead she killed my cat.

She killed my fish.

She killed my plants and my home.

She killed my world.

> "There is no death, only rebirth. If your world is dead, it is because you killed it."

I take a shallow breath and try not to think about it. I stop trying to get the clipboard and allow my arm to return to my side. Betrayed by my own body. Utterly betrayed. I hate myself in a way I don't remember ever experiencing before. If I could, I would hit myself. I would ball up my one good fist and smash myself into the oblivion I deserve.

Crush the mind that can't see past my truth. Crush the heart that would have me dead. Crush the weakness I am. Just crush the whole thing.

I want to leave. I want to die.

What have I done to deserve this hell? What did I say to Hellen that made her do this to me?

But, I know what I did. I told her the truth, and it made her insane.

I fall backwards in time and remember the recent close call with my stitches, and I realize for the first time even if I had managed to get my hand around the water glass, I wouldn't have been able to drink from it. I was not in any condition to do it.

That was the kind of truth Hellen faced, only instead of the truth of water, she was faced with the truth of her soul.

I told my wife she didn't exist, and she believed me. Her death was nothing more than a prophecy of self, fulfilled.

# 3
## JULY 9

Part of me remembers the real world. The world of logic and love. The place I used to rest my head when I was tired, the place where I used to run in the rain. I'm getting stronger, just a little, and as I do, part of me wants to return to the place outside of here.

Outside of my annihilation.

There isn't any real comfort in my life, unless I count the artificial love of the drugs. I'm not happy or positive. As I watch the world outside live its life without me, I'm holding on to the hope the doctors are telling the truth, that I'll eventually make a full recovery. They say they can justify such optimism simply because all of my injuries are minor when viewed individually.

They make a hell of a noise together though, I think to myself.

My left arm is working passably now, and I was able to write an awkward note asking for help to take care of my home. That's helped me a lot because as much as my life is a living hell, losing Franklin and my tanks in such a cruel way would have made the damage so much worse. The nurses were actually quite amazing, really. From my few scratches on the paper they realized what I wanted, and I was able to guide them through the phone book, pointing out the people they could call for help.

Getting my plants watered and Franklin fed was actually pretty easy in the end. They called my boss and asked if he could stop by my home and do the work. He was fine with the idea of helping one of his own, and I was relieved to hear later Franklin was at the vet's office, skinny and tired, but with proper nourishment he would be fine. It had been almost nine days, but he had made it.

As for the tanks and my plants, things hadn't gone so well.

Most of my smaller plants had died from a lack of water and light. I keep the shades drawn after dusk, and the accident which put me here happened long after I would have normally been in bed. The larger plants looked like they might be salvageable, at least according to my boss, and all I can guess is size matters, at least for plants. The tanks were gone though, just finished, and nothing was going to save them.

Marine tanks are not easy to maintain, and although I don't know exactly what happened, I can guess. The artificial ecosystem became unstable somehow, maybe too much protein in the water, or more likely a small fish died from lack of food. One small rotting body would quickly poison the tank. The bacteria feeding on death would cause the oxygen levels to crash, and the remaining corals and fish would have smothered.

Two worlds destroyed, unremarked and without witnesses. My fish had no names, so I'll mourn their loss alone.

Trying not to think of my life before this place is making me tense. I find my thoughts drawn back, against my will and better judgement, to my life before the accident. Held fast, lying on my back, stretched by wires and wrapped for company, I've nothing else to do but work hard at keeping sane. How was I able to function before this? I think of the things I did every day as if they were impossible. My body did the work and I fed it. That was the deal, and it was going along just great. Hellen, that miserable word, seemed happy to be with me, at least until I killed her, and the space that image takes in my thoughts is immense. Impossible. It couldn't have been as easy as I remember it.

We lived in one of her family's more modest homes, six bedrooms on twenty acres, and when she asked me to leave, I suppose she did it to protect herself from me. The day I left, both of us supervising heavy men abusing my things into a crude looking van, we tried not to be cruel about it.

*"If I had wanted to be cruel I could have been. Easily."*

"Leave me alone." I respond quietly.

Hellen came from a very wealthy family. She was a senior banking executive of indeterminate job description, at a level where applications are less important than breeding. She made more money than most people can comprehend and she wasn't aware, at any level, the family money that came before her had made it possible. She always thought, and was never afraid to say, the people who didn't do as well as she were somehow just not trying hard enough. Homeless people were homeless because they were lazy. Families were broke and the elderly lacked proper care simply because they had not been frugal enough. It was never because the system had been so obviously skewed against them. Against us all. She couldn't see it. It was because of this background when she looked at me, even as far back as the time we dated, I could see she 'understood' my choice of career to be far beneath her.

I drove a bus.

Really blue collar stuff, and really difficult to explain to someone with her upbringing. She always told me she thought I was above the job, and I suspect she said it to convince herself she had chosen a worthy mate. If I had chosen to drive a bus for reasons other than some sort of noble self-depreciation it would have reflected badly on her, at least in her eyes, and more importantly in the eyes of her family.

In hindsight, I think our getting together was a compensation tactic on her part, and a symptom of apathy on mine. I know she saw me in the same delusional light as any one of a hundred random magazine articles, each of them describing in envious tones some bored stockbroker abandoning his wealth and stature to do something romantic and menial.

"I gave up all that money to drive this little boat in the Caribbean, guiding tourists through this beautiful coast," the newly liberated millionaire says in the interview.

They never mention he used millions of his dollars to set up his little escape, and they never mention the millions sitting dusty but loved under his mattress. I was Hellen's way of telling herself she wasn't one of the affected rich. She was in touch with the common person, so much so, she even married one. The fact she made herself believe I wasn't common, in spite of all the evidence to the contrary, well, that's what delusional means.

For my part, my apathy allowed me to not care. I saw a rich, beautiful woman who seemed to love me, and I was too young to realize her wealth and her heart would never really be mine.

Thinking about this isn't easy, and in the most unhealthy sense I've been mulling the days of my life with her in my skull, like rocks in a tumbler, for days. The memories and the emotions are wearing smooth, rolling more and more quietly together, and they are becoming more beautiful each time I examine them. Removed from reality and removed from time, they seem somehow better than just emotions, better than just memories. They are becoming smooth and clean, and no trace of blood or tears or soil or sand remains.

> "We were a miracle. You were on vacation and I was travelling for work. The two of us so far from home, surrounded by millions of strangers, and yet we found ourselves together in the same small cafe. We ordered coffee as a couple for the first time that morning, and we fell in love. Our joining was beautiful. You can't say otherwise."

I open my eyes, pulling myself back from my introspections, and look outside. The time of day seems unimportant and I'm surprised by the sun. My eyes start to water, causing my vision to blur for a few seconds. The gruesome smell of my bandages, my consciousness trapped by an odour, makes it hard for me to look outside without tearing up.

Since I arrived last week, the park hasn't changed, but I see it more clearly for what it is, a small ecosystem struck and minted in the middle of a busy city. The birds and the squirrels, the crows and the dogs and the cats, all of them living with people, feeding off our scraps, walking and living and mating and dying, with us on the hill.

My eyes are full of quiet tears as I watch the world happen on the hill. I can't go there, not yet, but I can try to picture the person I will be when I do. The impossible person in my future who is above this crap. The hero who will not hate this artificial world with its pain and its drugs. The person who will be able to recognize his insanities and love them for what they are.

They will be me.

Right now, the smell of these bandages is keeping me in this room, in my cell, in this rank and broken body I can't use without suffering. The walls smell of rotting wounds. When I pull my chin down painfully to look at my swollen, purple legs, I can also see minute spots of blood on the bed rail by my feet.

When I think about my time with Hellen, it sends me to a dark place. Crucified to my bed in this temple of blood. I'm told I'll live again, but until I do, Hellen's memory will keep me lodged in this rankest pit of hell. I used to love her in my own way, but the golden dagger prods deeper into my heart, and the temple of blood is vibrating.

Like so many couples, we used to enjoy our talks.

*"I still do."*

Once, soon after I began to openly discuss my new-found atheism, I told her the weekly confessions of her church were just a big religious lie, and she should come to terms with the fact a truly moral person wouldn't need to be threatened by a god in order to want to do good, or to desire being moral or just. I called it owning our evil, and when I suggested the idea she should somehow own the evil she did, that she should be personally responsible for her unjust hatreds and her unfair derisions, she stopped me cold. 'This sort of nonsense will not be entertained' was how she phrased it. It was just a few days later we had the fatal conversation. Just a few days until I said the words that killed her.

Hellen had come home from work quite upset. Large protests were happening outside her office tower, led by people who wanted some accountability from her bank. They demanded an open accounting of the bank's actions and they demanded restitution for the results. Hellen understood the issues, not surprisingly considering she helped make the decisions. She knew she didn't have a moral leg to stand on. She also understood better than most, the bank's well-documented history of financial actions against the interests of common humanity. Eventually, the police had to be called to clear a path, allowing her staff into the building.

As she was ferried through the crowd behind large shields and even larger men, the accusations hurled at her by the protesters struck her as naive and silly. On her way home, Hellen visited her church, and when she returned home later that evening, we spoke of what happened. She tore into the people who had been so publicly angry with her.

"You can't expect people to be perfect all the time, as if we lived in some sort of Utopian fantasy," she began.

"People are callous and mean, and they will steal and lie to get what they want all the time. We all sin, we all fail at being good, and you have to forgive them those sins, otherwise there would be no hope of salvation for anyone," she said.

Without any warning my face reddened. Without thought or filters, I spoke from my heart. I became angry, at her specifically, and not just her point of view. I heard her words and they became nothing more than a scripted cop-out. A way for her to excuse the bad behaviours of bad people. The bank Hellen worked for was well known for its brutality in the name of its capitalist ambitions, and even better known for its lack of concern for the consequences of its actions. She wanted to add a layer of religion in some vain effort to excuse herself and her company? The arrogance of it made me want to scream. The protesters were not the ones doing the evil, but somehow that was what I was being asked to believe. I wouldn't have it. I told her if she wasn't comfortable with what she'd done, then that was her moral quagmire to resolve. I told her she shouldn't paint the innocent victims as bad people, simply because they wanted her company to behave morally. As I spoke, her anger grew, and as the angry moments passed, I could see her building the next justifications in her mind.

I saw then, the truth of her argument. She didn't care about the justifications or the rationalizations. They were unimportant. The reality was, she simply saw me and anyone who opposed her as stupid. As beneath her. She assumed anyone not on her side was an idiot.

She was on the side of faith, and nothing more needed to be said.

I opened the bomb-bay doors, and let fly the first of my many assaults on her immortal soul.

"People are not perfect, I never said they were, but when you screw up you have to understand the evil you perpetrated, the wrong you created, was a creation of your own. God did not make you do bad things, you did. If you steal a mortgage from a family for profit, you did not abrogate your will to anyone, and you haven't been guided by some mythical hand. When I hurt the woman I love by telling you this, I do it by my own free will, hopefully for our mutual gain, and with my own desire to not be harshly judged. However, when your immoral actions are discovered, when they are exposed and judged, you have to remember only you did the wrong, nobody else. Not your parents, not your peers, and most certainly not any sort of god.

"The society we live in must deal with you, just as the protesters are dealing with your company. If our society is healthy, if our culture is not corrupted, then you can expect to be forgiven. Restitution will be expected, but in the end, if you are to return to society as a productive member, forgiveness must be assured and it must be absolute. Did you imagine somehow only a church goer can forgive? Seriously, forgiveness is not a unique or absolute product of the religious mind. Those protesters are right. You and your company are in the wrong, and nothing but your actions from this day forward will change that. If you and your banker friends want to rejoin decent society, you will all need to stop. To expect forgiveness before then is delusional."

Her heart stopped at that moment.

My legs hurt, and I can't hear the birds through the smell.

# 4 JULY 14

The surgery to find out what collapsed my lung was today and it went well. They removed a splinter of bone from a broken rib which apparently caused all the trouble. I could breathe better this afternoon once the anaesthetic wore off than the day my lung collapsed. I still can't look down well enough to see, but I'm told the scar is quite small, with only seven stitches.

When I was a kid seven stitches would have given me demigod status in school. Now it's considered a minor hiccup in my day.

I was surprised when my nurse showed me a photograph of the splinter. It was much smaller than I would have guessed, certainly much smaller than the stiletto it forced between my ribs each time I tried to breathe without tears. They say it was literally pointing sideways, directly into the layer of tissue that surrounds the lungs. The Pleural sac. All I knew from my little spot in hell was I couldn't take a deep breath, I couldn't cry, I couldn't do much of anything until they drained the gore that filled the place my lung was supposed to be.

Morning ablutions took on a whole new meaning for me. A person doesn't easily forget a tube in his side releasing cupfuls of odiferous hot blood plasma every morning. I won't miss that, now that I can begin the process of forgetting it ever happened.

A nurse offered me my first meal since I arrived, a chocolate flavoured nutrition drink, and she was very good about feeding me. I've never been fed before, and if I wasn't so helpless I might have actually enjoyed it a bit more. The drink itself was delicious, and if it was chalky I didn't care. As I worked hard to swallow each small sip, my stomach tight after two weeks of inactivity, the nurse kept playing with her hair. Some sort of french braid she was constantly adjusting as she held my straw. Watching her the entire time she was helping me, I was human and connected. After I finished eating she placed a bedpan under the day table. She did it just before she left, in the same way someone would turn off the lights.

Hospitals are about habits.

I am literally being held, partly suspended over my bed by threaded bolts which go through what's left of my bones. Those bones are being pulled straight by the bolts, which are in turn being pulled by straps, which are then connected to cables, and those cables are attached to weights. It would take bolt cutters and a lot of morphine to get me out of this bed. It should be easy to understand why not one slight deviation from the usual routine has ever been detected by me, not in the two weeks I've been awake.

Awake, drugs, sleep, awake, turn white from the pain, drugs, sleep, awake, grind my teeth in pain, lights out, drugs, sleep.

The nights tend to be less eventful.

I'm beginning to distrust habits. After Hellen and I had our first little talk (the one where I let her know I wasn't going to be her soft shoulder to cry on whenever her bad behaviour started to cause her problems) it was almost as if a habit had been created after just the one event.

Our talks, during which we used to have a great time discussing some pretty weighty topics, went badly downhill. I became the self-appointed finder of her intellectual flaws, and the flaws I found (my intellectual bread and butter) always focused around her two religions: money and the church. Each of them provided her with a myriad of moral blind spots, which I was able to weave into and out of as I took my shots at her. As I dissected her spiritual corpse.

If a man ever deserved to be killed by his victim, I suppose it was me.

After more assaults on her spirituality than I care to remember, Hellen knew very well I was not going to capitulate to her beliefs any longer. Our last big talk ended when I belligerently explained to her morality, forgiveness, compassion, altruism, all of the great and noble states of the human condition were in fact just that - traits of humans. In doing so, I lost her completely. To her, these traits were the direct result of being pious and well-bred, while I saw them as traits that were co-opted. Taken, then corrupted to serve the wants of small and dangerous men.

"The bastards own your soul, and they expect you to pay rent!" As I spoke the words, I could see her flinch. From her point of view, my attitude was heresy.

"It is."

She was gone to me from that moment on, but even if I had noticed, I couldn't act. Speaking those words, hearing myself voice them to her, something had changed in me as well. Something had been awakened.

I never actually told her that night (she might well have died an even more tragic death if I had) but as I tore into her for the last time, as my attempted destruction of her personal illusion came to its climax, even greater ideas were forming in my mind. They came to me with a speed and certainty I still can't explain, and as the final, fatal words came from my mouth, as I sent the last volley of canon fire into the bow of her spiritual ship, I realized fully and completely a person who worships a religion could never be as noble or as just as a person who did not. The reason was simple and elegant.

Her churches and her cash - they were her filters on the world, on the universe, and the reality of it we all share. They would never allow her to see honesty, or faithfulness, or anything good about us as people. She couldn't see it because her beliefs tainted the colours of the real world, giving everything she saw a wash of her beliefs, altering their shades to match and conform to the beliefs she had been taught since her birth. Everything she saw was tinged. A shade applied that was untrue. Nothing of her view could be honest. Nothing could be truthful. Not her motives, not the results of her actions. It was all filtered through the mental obligations of her wealth, of her piety.

As I voiced those final parting words I could see, without those filters, everything was sharper. Brighter. A person's good was more pure, and because we own our evil, a person's evil became an even greater blight on themselves and our species. Without the filters, without the ideologies they perpetuated, a person was liberated to see the world as it was. The universe became both larger and more real. Time had meaning and the little yellow bird on the branch outside my window, who I still see from time-to-time, can exist along side me as an equal. I can react to him with a truth that would be impossible if I saw him as less than myself.

I'm different, of course, but more? A lack of filters say no, just different.

My first atheist thoughts eventually brought me to a place where I pitied Hellen, but they seemed right. That was enough.

Thinking back to the day of the protest, I know a part of me also died. How could it have not? The ideas, the direction they would clearly be taking me, they were new to me, and I wasn't expecting them. They were so immediate, so obvious and scary for their novelty. I've always been content to allow life to happen. I was easy to please ... but this line of thought took hold of me, the feeling of freedom I couldn't even explain ... I found myself wanting to follow up. I wanted to be a part of this scary new world I was imagining.

I think my old self took one look at where I was headed and simply stopped breathing.

To this day, understanding the limitations placed on her by her religion and her cash, I still can't think of any way she could have been the better of me as a person. Not one. Her enormous wealth allowed her to buy far more than I ever could, and she had so many friends she even hired staff to manage her relationships with them, but as far as what was good for the human race? During our talks I started to feel she was dangerous, in a way I didn't yet comprehend. I became aware a small part of me was afraid of her, and because I didn't fully understand why, it confused me.

Of course, judging by the lovely purple and red colour of my two legs bolted to the bed in front of me, I was right to be afraid. If she had been told to put the whole of humanity into the car with us that night, to protect her beliefs, I'm not sure she wouldn't have done it.

We all live with our fantasy of the end, of our own personal apocalypse, and I know hers had been bred into the bone. She was taught to play her role in one way only, and her great tragedy was she didn't even know she was just acting.

Give me chocolate carbohydrates through a straw and suddenly I can think. I've been awake for two weeks, and I can see I'm slowly healing. I'm still insane, but it's starting to feel like the good kind of insanity. The kind that can make friends.

Habits are dangerous things, especially in the herd. When everyone follows them, as they do here in the hospital, the habit becomes invisible. Nobody sees them. They become the shadows of our intellect, kept in a small envelope in the basement, easily forgotten but so important. I can see it all the time in this place. The staff rush by doing the important work of important people, and at no point does it appear to dawn on anyone they are repeating the same important work they did just minutes before. The older nurses, the ones who have already celebrated their first retirement only to return a year or two later, they understand. They are answering to the power of habit. The way it keeps you safe. The hard edge it keeps to your throat to motivate you, to make you work. But that's not its job. There might be such a thing as right and wrong, but it doesn't care. A habit's purpose is to be. Its measure is itself, always looking inwards towards its fulfilment.

Ideology and rhetoric are habits, and they are the enemies of rational thought. They are its enemy primarily because they look so much like it.

My legs are smaller, less swollen, and I'm feeling braver than I did even a few days ago. I know it's an illusion though. I know, nailed to this bed, in spite of everything I do to avoid it, eventually I'll become a child in pain, fearful and scared, eyes begging for the needle. Until then I'll enjoy this time. No tears, no anger.

There is such a thing as right and wrong, but our problem is its measure. No god, no economic rule, no mantra or religious doctrine can ever presume to tell us what is good. That can only be judged by one simple idea. If what we do is going to hurt our species, individually or as a whole, either directly or by wilfully damaging any part of this world we need to survive, then it is, by that measure, evil.

No filter will let that one through. Not ever.

## JULY 15 — 5

I've been thinking about Hellen today, and I wish I would stop. I'm tired of living in this past I seem determined to relive, tired of trying to understand something I want to forget. I wish I could become the bliss ignorance promises, but instead I'm finding myself brooding. Thinking in circles about why Hellen did this to me. I realize after our final conversation, on the day we separated, I left somewhat fearful of her, and yet I did nothing. I even entertained the idea we would eventually get back together.

Why?

I suspect it was a lack of imagination on my part. I couldn't believe one of the sophisticates, one of the financially blessed, was capable of such barbarism. My fears were apparently rooted in a place that understood us as a species far better than I. If I had listened to my instincts I might not be here today, in this morgue of personal identity.

My fear centered on that Orwellian ability of the religious and the rich to have two completely opposing viewpoints, yet somehow not be conscious of the conflict. It's something that bothered me in a vague sort of way my entire life, and it was hard for me to miss even as a child. Hellen had that ability, to think two opposing thoughts at once, and she used it all the time. When I witnessed it, the suddenness could take my breath away.

In our talks I tried pointing out those contradictions, those logical impossibilities she presented to me as debate, and eventually I gave up. She couldn't see them, and the more I pushed the more she fought to explain her rationalizations. It always ended in circular frustration for both of us, with our mutual anger unsatisfied, leaving each of us hotly anticipating the next battle. The last time it came up was when I presented my question to her regarding the impossible gun.

I've often wondered how those special religious fanatics, those terrible religious warriors who kill the innocent as a matter of pious duty, could reconcile their hatred and disbelief of the earthly world of science with their use of the technologies and tools those sciences create.

I asked Hellen directly, how does a person who sees the world as a recent creation of a god, and who is opposed to teaching their children about things scientific (even the most basic concepts such as evolution, for fear of polluting their minds) pick up a gun and use that deadly creation of our scientific knowledge to kill his enemy?

When I talked to her about it, I used the term 'Orwellian' deliberately. That ability to both see and not see simultaneously.

I argued a gun is not something that just spontaneously forms under a rock. It is perhaps one of the most eloquent examples of evolution ever created. Its existence begs the question of the technologies required to actually make a modern firearm. As it turns out, they are not inconsequential.

As usual, it always starts in the earth. In the rocks on which we live. The materials used to manufacture the gun have to be mined, so we need survey and mining technologies. Refining technologies, techniques to purify and isolate, must then be created to allow us to make those raw minerals into something useful. Once that is completed, metallurgy becomes important because no metal harvested directly from the earth, except a few rare and expensive examples, could withstand the forces a modern gun creates. So using the ideas metallurgy teaches us, we bring our base metals to a foundry to carry out the very non-intuitive science of alloying, and after all of this hard work, all we have at this point is a lump of very hard metal.

It should be mentioned foundries historically used coal as a source of fuel, and assuming our fanatic thinks the earth is only thousands of years old, the foundry ovens are therefore powered by a fuel that cannot exist.

Now to the machine shop. Lathes working in tolerances the human eye cannot even distinguish, made using even more exotic alloyed metals, carve the lump of metal into a finished gun. Mechanical engineering technologies, of the type that created those curious automatons of the nineteenth and twentieth centuries, have reached a level of perfection hard to imagine. A human hair is a clumsy and blunt object in comparison.

Are we done? Not even close. We built this gun, but how did it get designed?

To design a tool as advanced as a firearm one needs to understand the limits of what our alloyed metals can do, so technologies were created to allow us to test them. This would include the ability to microscopically x-ray solid metal parts looking for signs of stress. Once we understand the limits of what our metals can do, those mechanical engineers need to apply the theories of their craft to the functioning of this proposed tool, and once that's done, they communicate their designs to those who will construct them using one of our very oldest technologies.

Writing and drawing.

Of course, even that has progressed. We have evolved from cuneiform and glyph to technical drawing, which can take forms as familiar as the old-fashioned hand-drawn blueprints to the most modern three-dimensional computer-aided design images, or CAD drawings. Most people don't realize the majority of the cars we see every day in magazine ads are not the real item. They are computer-generated pictures taken directly from CAD files. The resulting images are so perfect, we can't tell the difference from real.

The gun is complete, and yet it's still a paperweight. We have forgotten the part that goes boom. That's chemistry, or alchemy as the church used to call it. With gunpowder, we finally reach a point where we have a tool that seems fully-functional, and yet what have we forgotten?

Aiming the damn thing. Trajectory technology, Newtonian mathematics really, and it was one of the primary motivators for the creation of the first computers as we know them today, such as ENIAC.

There we go. I presented that entire line of thought to her and then asked how someone could deny any of it exists? How could a person who does not believe in science deny they are surrounded by it?

"Of course it exists, God put it all there for us to use," was the only answer I could get from her.

Thousands of years of scientific inquiry, most of it done with the threat of death for heresy hanging over their heads, and Hellen reduced it to one line. As I said, she could take my breath away.

Perhaps, in hindsight, it wasn't overlooked. Perhaps it was simply being used to enforce a moral measure not in keeping with good and evil as I now see it. In the same way a person uses a computer without knowing about binary number systems, or drives a car without understanding internal combustion, the religious simply use the gifts of science. Use the scientific gifts given to them by thousands of years of (mostly atheist) thought and discovery. In the case of the gun, they use those gifts to kill us.

Perhaps we shouldn't enforce laws to keep guns away from children and the insane. Perhaps we should instead create laws to keep guns away from saints and prophets, and their followers.

# 6
## JULY 16

The window has saved me more times than I care to count. I watch as the world spins along in the park, and I hope for visits from my yellow friend. My medical captivity has been an experience I am finding difficult to translate into words, it is so foreign to what I've known before, and yet, as I said last week, the routines assert themselves so quickly my head reels every time I think of it.

The protein drinks are making me feel strong. Really strong. My good arm is able to carry water to my lips, and I'm able to write clearly enough the game of charades I've been playing with the nurses is becoming a memory. My neck is starting to feel better as well, and this has given me a better view of my room, and all the goodies in it.

First, there is that rolling bedside table. It leans over me, being useful as it should, not straying from where it's supposed to be. My good arm can manoeuvre it forward and back, allowing me a bit of perceived freedom. I say perceived, because I'm still tied to the bed in traction.

Looking forward, over my discoloured legs and through the weights and pulleys, sits my dresser. Two drawers with a few small pots of flowers on top. My nurse read the messages to me. They are mostly from acquaintances, like my boss who rescued Franklin. She tells me the largest bunch is from work. I could have guessed. The bouquet is standard issue human resources get-well-fare, so I know if I look for a signature, all I'll find is a Transit logo along with the obligatory stamped signature from the CEO. I think it's pretty funny he would try to take back thousands of dollars of my wages through a war on my union, but somehow still feel completely OK sending me flowers. He's certainly not a friend, in fact I don't think I've ever met the man, so why send me such a shallow gift? I suppose his religion told him to. Seeing them sitting on the dresser under the window, I wonder who they were supposed to make feel better?

I can't help but grin at that thought.

I also have a television. The man in biological hell, with wires pulling him this way and that, has a television. I see them as our modern replacement for the telescope, but with a caveat: they usually only allow us to view artificial worlds. The nurse told me if I want to watch anything I'll need to pay a weekly fee, which made me laugh. The TV itself is a small one, the old kind with a picture tube, and it's folded (mostly flat) against the wall. It sits on the end of a telescopic arm, and if I were to ask they would pull it out, allowing me to mentally unplug, drooling medicated serenity into the idiot box.

I know better though. Since I arrived, I've come to realize morphine is much better for that. Television, in all of its blue phosphorous glory, is for amateurs. To gain admission into this cult of calm, the staff demands commitment from their followers. The kind of commitment only a syringe can deliver.

I'm grinning again. What an idea. Me talking about my appreciation of pharmacological bliss. I'm the guy everyone knows will only drink a beer if I don't have to work the next day, and yet here I am, getting drugs from a needle. The hardcore stuff too, right in the fattest part of my ass. It feels raw from the number of times they've loaded me up down there, and I just hope the sum total of all those injections won't leave some sort of pin cushion scar.

Scars. I forgot about that.

Obviously I haven't had a chance to stand in front of a mirror, so I can't actually say what scars I'm going to take away from my stay in this church of the blessed sphincter. From what I'm feeling though, I can guess. There is going to be a huge scar over my hip where the glove box went, and I'm still trying to figure that one out. Then, there are the smaller scars on both my legs. Some of them will result from the threaded rods through my bones that hold me in traction, and some of them are already healing from where the car managed to push its way through me. Judging from my injuries, my best guess as to how I got most of those is I was somehow pressed under the glove box, legs first. The easiest way I've found to envision this was to imagine myself crawling into the foot well, with my mid section on the seat and turned slightly to one side, my head, shoulders, back and arms pressed against the door. What a thought!

My right arm is a mess. It is still completely wrapped up, and they tell me I may need some minor skin grafts. Each of my fingers has it's own little splint, and they are clearly trying to force my hand to heal into something I can use again. They had said all my injuries were minor, but I really question what that's supposed to mean. I'm looking at a hand that should probably have been hacked off at the scene of the accident. It's swollen too, even after all this time, so the small parts of my fingers showing through the bandaging don't look like fingers - more like raw sausage. I'm getting a chill just looking at them.

Staying here, seeing my injuries and feeling how I feel, is hard on the head. As the nurses work on me they talk, mostly to themselves, about how I'll be fine. That may be so, but that's not what's been giving me the hardest time. It's the smell. The damn smell is so overpowering, I can't think from the distraction. What makes it worse is the knowledge the smell causing me so much distress is actually me. Not my injuries, not this place, but my new normal self.

My scent is completely different, and it's revolting.

In my frustration I scribbled a note to a nurse, asking her where the smell is coming from. After she made sure none of my wounds had gone septic, she realized what I was talking about. She said it was the drugs.

It seems when you pump dose after dose of antibiotics, pain killers, and who knows what else into a person, a body has to get rid of it somehow. Most of it comes out in our urine, but some of it comes out in our pores. In our skin.

This hospital, in the name of saving me, has invaded my body with steel, my mind with routine, and the rest of me with drugs. The holy trinity of the blood healers, making me well by changing and owning me.

I smell disgusting, and it makes me cry.

It might seem obvious, but I'm still finding my emotions very hard to control. I fool myself into thinking I've gotten over Hellen, at least on some sort of surface level that let's me think about her. That emotional fantasy evaporates when I'm faced with the truth of my behaviour. One minute I find myself thinking dispassionately, objectively, about the elements of our life together, and the next? I can't even remember the colour of her hair without completely breaking down.

She was a blond when I met her, but she started to dye her hair brunette within a couple of years. She explained to me, in her very matter of fact sort of way, the people she worked with saw blonds as sluts. From her descriptions of the various company outings she was required to participate in, I would have to take that description one level further. Her bosses, and she had many, made sure the prostitutes they hired to accompany them were always curvy, willing, and above all ... blond. Hellen dyed her hair because she was tired of looking like the main course in the company bimbo buffet.

Put that way, I can't say I blame her.

I find it funny to think about. I remember the stories she told to me, usually during one of her weirdly vulnerable, sherry-lubricated, evening confessionals. The sins of her co-workers laid bare and exposed to my criticism, and somehow I never thought to ask her why she stayed with the company. I knew the pay was more than good, it was actually obscene, but to be treated that way, even indirectly, seemed like such a huge compromise. I don't think I could have done it. One afternoon, while we were out shopping, I remember asking her what she liked about her job. Her answer surprised me.

She liked it because everyone who worked there was a 'family person.'

Seriously. She said it with a straight face. I didn't ask again.

I think she saw herself as a family person, or at least she wanted to. We never had kids. Hellen miscarried three times, but she always imagined if she could just carry to term, she would be a wonderful mother. I could see it in her eyes. I wasn't as convinced, and I always wondered if she would put our kids on the company payroll, just to make sure she could reliably book a meeting with them twice-monthly. Once, while discussing the possibility of trying to have a baby, and thinking I was being funny, I told her. The anger it brought out of her shocked me.

I thought she was going to punch me.

In hindsight, I'm just glad I recognized it as quickly as I did and made amends right away. She calmed down eventually, but I never again dared question how good a mother I thought her schedule and her work would allow her to be.

Her cash and her church. They each made their demands on her life and her time, and like all religions they don't tolerate unbelievers graciously.

I'm feeling my legs now. The pain is always there, but after a while it starts to get distracting. I know I only have a few more minutes of relative comfort left before the waiting game starts. That's when I slowly shut down all the higher functions and start the process of living through it. Deep breaths and progressively louder curses in my mind, at least until the next shot of morphine arrives. I can't hear my next door neighbour yet, but if I'm feeling it I'm guessing he is too. We have definitely kept a bizarre synchronicity about our pain I suspect speaks volumes to either the efficiency of the staff, or the fact we are both listed in the restricted meds list. It's easier and faster to do the paperwork and prepare the two doses at the same time, rather than signing off on each one separately.

Whatever, at this point I don't really care. I'm waiting to give my offering, the golden gluteus maximus of persistent pain, and the chickens are dancing in the streets. Dancing in my veins and in my muscles. It really is hard to think straight when your body starts to speak to you in razor blade and knife dialects.

The breathing helps a bit, so I just keep at it and try to get lost in the rhythm. It's never perfect, and I spend almost as much time trying to get my focus back on my breathing as actually feeling any sort of minor relief, but that little bit makes the rest much easier to take, so I breathe.

Breathe in, breathe out. Breathe in and count to four, breathe out and count to eight. Back and forth. In and out. Blue and yellow and red and yellow and green and blue and yellow and ... shit this helps ... and yellow ... fuck ... and blue.

Man, it's getting tight.

I always try not to speak. I try not to vocalize in any way when the pain starts to get out of control, because I imagine that would only make it worse. I also think I would die of embarrassment if I were to cry out, yelling like some sort of idiot, which I think is about the stupidest thing yet in this place. I'm the fractured little man who feels emotion, and I care enough for the comfort of others I don't want to impose my suffering on them.

> *"Suffering is good for the soul. I think you would do well with a great deal more."*

"What the hell would you know about suffering, Hellen?"

Next door starts to moan. Yeah, we're both there now.

He doesn't know I'm here, at least I don't think he does, and so I feel like I have an advantage. I hear him cry, his shouts and his curses, and I use them as a surrogate for my own pain. I can contain my outside by allowing his pleas to be mine. We are sharing this violation of our bodies together, but only one of us has the company and solace of an accomplice.

We are both prisoners who will eventually leave this cult of blood ... fucking nurses who are taking their damn time to get the papers done ... and when we do, perhaps I'll find him and we can relate our times here to each other.

Broken men and their broken souls, talking shop.

What can I do to stop this? I feel like the muscles are trying to leave my body, swelling and bloating in their effort to dislodge themselves. The blood vessels cursing the captivity of the flesh and trying to escape however they can. The pull. It's so hard on my brain. I feel like I can't stop the screaming from coming. It happens so fast, and it stays for so long. The nurses won't be by with the drugs for at least another half an hour, and I'm almost dead. I won't make it till then.

Oh man, why can't I just die? All I need is a brick and some leverage. This is not what a human is suppose to face, this is not a normal life.

We were never designed to suffer like this.

"And how are we doing today?" the nurse asks routinely. She doesn't expect a response.

She is here to deliver the pain medication to 4b, and the patient is held rigid in his bed in a frame of grey aluminum rods and thin steel wire. She is in no hurry as she checks his pulse, his blood pressure, his breathing. He has broken a sweat today, more than normal, and his brow seems to be wet and spongy when she wipes it. She notes it in his chart, and it confirms the pattern from her previous entries. He isn't reacting well to morphine. Nothing serious, but he might need to be weaned earlier than normal.

The syringe is on the bedside table, and if she had cared to look she would see he was staring at it, desperate, animal lust in his eyes. He is barely holding on, but she doesn't see it.

Content with his vitals, she unceremoniously pulls up the thick open weave blanket and exposes his backside to the air. He is not able to turn, so she leans down to get a better look at his ass and plants the needle squarely into the deepest part of the muscle. A professional pull back on the plunger, and then she quickly empties its contents into him.

The needle comes out, and with a quick flick of the wrist she breaks the point off into a yellow sharps bin. It's a bio-hazard now, and the staff must be protected from it.

Adjusting her braid, she looks down at him for the first time today, possibly the first time since he arrived so long ago. She wonders if she knows him. He looks familiar, at least as familiar as a swollen and distorted person can in this position.

It must be his eyes, she thinks, they seem familiar.

She stands over his body as it heals, just for a minute, and she can see the drug taking hold of him. The effect always intrigues her. His eyes lose focus almost right away, and within seconds he is asleep and oblivious. If she were to check his blood pressure again, she would see it was down quite significantly.

"You're not going to be happy if we cut your dose, I can see that."

The patient and the walls are both oblivious to her comment.

The door opens, the door closes. Silence returns to the room. Outside, a yellow bird sits on a branch just a few feet from the window, and every once in a while it makes a sound that gently pushes the veil back. Each note ends quickly, and afterwards the tubes and the wires rush to rejoin the stillness, while the floor doesn't even notice the sound at all. The man on the bed is dreaming of fish and cars and boats and his bird.

His manly bird, and outside the manly bird makes the sounds of prideful noise it loves.

# 7 JULY 17

I had a paper and pen chat with the doctor today and I'm guessing things will be a bit weird for a while. It seems I'm showing symptoms that suggest I'm not tolerating the morphine well. Early signs of dependence, odd skin reactions, blood pressure too low, generally the kinds of things they don't like to see in the patients they care for. They tell me none of it is very serious, but they want to change my dose. The goal is to keep my pain under control, while getting the dosage down to a level my body can handle.

My head says that sounds smart, but not my gut, and I'm sweating as I think about it.

I feel like they are playing a game with me. They give me these soul-killing drugs, and then just when they start to work I'm told they will be taking them away.

I'm getting better every day, but this talking about the pain killers is really scary. I don't know how I can face the pain I still feel every second of every day without something to numb it down. To take the edge off. They say they'll reduce the dose gradually, but I don't feel comforted.

I feel like I'm holding on to my self control by a thread, and they plan on cutting it.

My father was an intellectual and an addict, starting way back in the sixties when it was still cool to be that sort of thing. He was the prototypical hippie hedonist, and by the time I was born his philosophy was to do as many drugs as his body would allow, for as long as it would allow it. He followed that philosophy until his body stopped. The fact he made it past twenty five was a testament to the power of the human body to heal itself. The fact he made it to sixty five was an even greater shock to anyone who knew him, and I include myself in that pile.

He was a brilliant idiot and he didn't give a shit about anything, especially himself.

My mother was from the same small one church town and she was the brains in the marriage. Not to say she wasn't a major hippie acid-dropper like he was, she just knew when it was time to let the liver swelling go down a bit. It didn't save her though. They died within months of each other, each of them in their sixties; each of them from liver cancer.

The two of them together must have been an amazing sight when they were young. They were an impressive couple, if somewhat addled, even before they died. He was big and aggressive, often for no other reason than he wanted to indulge a need to bully someone ideologically, and she had an imagination that could fix time and show you the gears. I read some of her poetry, I was about twelve, and it traumatized me. I'm guessing it still affects me. It sure as hell changed me back then.

My mom was a hedonist, just like dad. She was also a stereotypical hippie and a heavy drug user. Thankfully for me, she did manage to clean herself up somewhat, and as she aged beyond her teenage bloom, she realized she could fake respectability well enough to get and keep a job. Eventually some good ones. However, aside from her drug use, she did carry one thing from those early hedonist years with her into adulthood, and eventually right into her old age.

She wrote, and very successfully sold, her poetry.

Her highly-graphic, highly-descriptive, highly-imaginative, pornographic poetry.

Years later, when I was in my early twenties, I was in the unfortunate position of having to describe my mom's writing to a friend. This girl I had just met recognized my mom's name from a few books she owned. I told this potential girlfriend my mom was like all the hippies back then - they were always out trying to find themselves. The only difference was that when my mom did find herself, she put a vibrator on it.

The girl laughed, and I blushed. The humorous truth in what I said reached deep into my youth. It reached downward into my most personal depths, those hopefully lost chasms in the deepest part of my psyche. Depths I had hoped at the time would never be plumbed. It was a joke that carried the weight of a century of psychoanalytic study and a seemingly endless trail of sticky tissues, carefully hidden under my mattress.

My mom's poetry traumatized me because I eventually found myself using it as ... how can I say this gently?

Wank material.

Freud would be proud. It was almost a relief when they died.

So here I am, trapped in this abattoir, knowing very soon I'll be begging the universe for the very thing I know did so much damage to my family and my childhood, and I decide to recount the decline and fall of my parents.

My messed up family life. We learn our lessons in spite of what we have.

I don't really have any clue what a normal family is, considering my own experience. I had the mom and dad, and we even had the occasional open-minded dog, but was that supposed to be normal? Judging from the stories I remember hearing from my friends in high school and college, my experience did seem to be somewhat less exceptional than I might have guessed, but was it still anything worth protecting?

This thing I'm facing with the hospital drugs, a part of me knows I'm already hooked. If they let me, I'll happily keep taking whatever chemical nirvana they offer once every four hours, until a vital organ gets tired of the abuse and dies. I've lived my whole life in fear of becoming my dad, a once formidable intellect turned dead head, his uniqueness killed by his own shaking hand, or my mom, who lost her moral centre so badly she wrote lyrical ballads of herself giving blowjobs, eventually earning a living from it. I know where my road goes, so in spite of an impending addiction, in spite of the fear malignant and sharp growing in the pit of my brain, I want the doctors and the nurses to keep me away from it. To change it. Make me forget it, so when I do get out of here I won't find myself talking to overconfident men in khaki shorts and flip-flops, assholes sipping lattes and talking about how worldly they are, while I make a deal with them for hundreds of dollars worth of some dead guys meds.

I saw my dad do that once, and it hurt my childish soul forever to realize how low he really was.

Families shouldn't be like that.

Hellen and I spoke of my family at times, but as far as she was concerned my parents simply reinforced her stereotype of working class intellectuals. Two humans, broken, written off. Eventually it was obvious there would be no solace in her company on the issue, but as we spoke of family it became clear, as much as she would have denied it, she came from a family as dysfunctional as mine.

She came from money. Lots of it, and they were a clan of solid church goers. A person could be forgiven for thinking she had a clearer understanding than most on the topic of family. A perfect and inspiring view of what good family is. Having lived those values. Having learned what those values were all about. Of course, she had no clue.

Short version: her father was morbidly workaholic, and he was extremely proud of the fact he made more money each successive year he was alive. Hellen saw him about once a week for most of her pre-adult life, and when they met, usually over ice cream or haute couture, his self-imposed duty was to brutally chastise her for whatever failings he could detect. His unthinking harshness was supposed to motivate her to achieve great things. Then there was the tragedy that was her mother. She was the bored housewife, that fantastic fantasy of pizza delivery boys and plumbers, revered and celebrated in sit-coms and romance novels. It was an open secret among those with the power and wealth she craved she could be had for little more than a compliment. She drank a lot as well, usually at parties that left the walls reeking of stale scotch and angry sex, but that didn't define her. Her desire to sample males, any and all males with the authority and gravitas to turn her head, was the thing she would have wanted marked on her tombstone.

Family? Hellen knew what it meant less than I did.

> "Such arrogance! How could you possibly expect to understand my family, when you have denied yourself membership into the greatest family in the world?"

I'm feeling dizzy a lot, lately. I should probably spend less time thinking about things that upset me.

This feels weird.

# 8
## JULY 19

My next door neighbour with the exploded leg had company yesterday. A lot of company. If I had to guess I would say probably fifteen adults and at least six kids. It sounded like some sort of family event had been planned, a reunion most likely, and the family from out of town descended on his room in full force to catch up and wish him well.

They were immediately disappointed.

I didn't know this, but the hospital enforces a strict three visitor limit. With just over twenty people visiting, there were problems. They eventually worked it out, but I thought the solution was a bit odd. Instead of allowing the visitors to stay for a short while, they had them play a sort of visitor tag team. Three family members at a time would each spend about fifteen minutes in his room with him, after which, the next round of family would take their place. The group ended up being there for almost three hours, laboriously cycling through tired and anxious adults as they tried in vain to entertain the bored kids. The system was setup after a five minute discussion with the nurse, and I unwillingly heard it all. How could I not? With that many people in negotiation over something as important as visitation rights, the volume went up even though tempers didn't.

People can only be so quiet when standing in the presence of so many other people ... who can only be so quiet.

That made sense.

I'm feeling rough and short-tempered. It's been two days since they reduced my dose, and I'm not happy about it. I'm in a lot more pain, which I suspect is obvious to anyone who looks at me. To make my time here even more fun, I find I'm pretty much in a constant state of anxiety waiting for that damn needle. They are giving me pills to help me relax, but the pills aren't helping. The blinds are open again today, but the bright morning sunlight is bothering me, it's making my eyes sore from squinting, so I lay in bed. Tense. Listening to the room and the ward.

I overheard the doctor talking about me. They said I might be taken out of traction in another week or so, and as much as I look forward to the freedom of not being nailed to my bed, I am not at all interested in finding out what it will feel like to rest my broken limbs on this plastic hospital mattress. They throb and pulse like air horns at a soccer match. I don't want to be awake for this. I wish they could make it stop.

I know this is for the best, but I don't care. I want them to get me back on a proper dose. An effective dose. Right now.

I noticed yesterday the noise from the visitors helped me forget myself for a while. The vicarious company of humans. I could fall into their voices and be a part of their intimate bond, part of those real people who still live in the real world. It didn't last though, and before long the distraction became the problem. Every fifteen minutes there was a new wave of hellos and goodbyes, people organizing the next exchange, and others making sure they hadn't been shorted for time. Their voices started to hurt, cutting into my thoughts and making me angry.

This whole affair with his visitors made it seem pretty obvious, from my vantage point anyway, this hospital is not very family-friendly. Imagine shunning family, in a place where it could be so useful. I know if I had someone, anyone, I would want them here by my side. All day, all night, to help me get through.

Would I deal with my pain differently if I had a son, if I had a daughter, to talk to?

At times, I'm very aware of my isolation, my solitude, and the staff of this hospital seems to prefer it this way. It's not a surprise to me, because I've always thought this idea applies to our whole society.

Hellen and I had it easy. Two incomes, one of them so high the word obscene was applicable, and childless. If the mood struck us we could drive small cars, or live in a small home, and because we consumed so few resources we would have small bills. But what about the men and women I worked with? The ones with kids?

An SUV isn't a political choice for them, it's a daily need.

Water bills that are pro-rated to reward the low user? They will never get the low rate. Bathing three kids, plus washing their clothes, makes that impossible. They face the same problem with heat, and electricity, and even access to the internet. All of it pro-rated to make sure families pay more than individuals.

A home? That white picket fence symbol of the affluence of North Americans? With stagnant wages and vastly inflated prices, slum rentals oftentimes become the only option.

Procreation without a trust fund has become a financial death sentence.

When did our culture decide hating the kids, or at least profiting from them, was so important?

I'm in so much pain I find it hard to engage my polite filter. This is a topic that's been mulling around in my head for years, and it was the subject that actually caused the most serious rift between myself and Hellen. At least it was, until I started the chain of events that brought me here.

The bank Hellen works with is pretty open about its dislike of children. After a few glasses of the dry white, she used to half-admit the worst thing she could do for her bank's reputation would be to show up pregnant. At some level I know she must have resented that, but for the sake of her share of the family empire she would never let on. Our fight started when she came home a bit flustered. She was upset because of a woman she had to fire.

I listened.

This woman apparently had to be let go. Hellen insisted nothing could be done about it, but the woman wasn't fired because she wasn't doing her job. Not at all. Instead, this woman was fired for having a second job. Of course, I asked why. Was she working for a competitor? Had she been caught divulging secrets? Hellen said no. She explained the woman was fired because she had three kids and she needed the extra cash to make ends meet. Hellen then explained to me, while she made herself a protein smoothie, having a staff member under that much financial stress made them targets, vulnerable to bribery and being manipulated.

I listened more attentively.

She explained, for reasons I can only guess, the studies her company had undertaken showed their wage structure was more than enough for a person to live on. The fact this woman chose to have a brood was entirely her fault, and Hellen couldn't see how the company should be expected to suffer for it.

She actually used the word brood.

Hearing this, I understood. The woman was fired because Hellen's company wasn't paying a living wage, and the bank didn't want to expose themselves to the downside of being the slumlord employer.

Hellen said, however obliquely, the woman was fired for having kids.

I stopped listening.

I work in a very blue collar job. I see the most marginalized members of our society every day, the people who are the very worst off. Over the years I've learned they all share something in common. However rough they look, however scrambled their minds have become, they are just tired and hungry people, trying against the odds to make ends meet every day. I try to help in my own small way. I give them free rides when they ask politely, I ignore the smell, and if they show up with a giant bag of bottles and cans during rush hour, I let them board whenever possible. Listening to Hellen explain her backwards attitude, watching her as she wore her complete lack of empathy for the woman's needs like some sort of twisted capitalist merit badge, caused me to speak more plainly than I ever had before. I wanted her to know just how callous and inhuman I thought she had become.

"Hellen," I began. "I sincerely hope you never decide to lower yourself enough to get a job at Transit. From what you just told me, you would fire half the people there, all the while claiming you were forced to do it. Then you would come home, pouting, feeling sorry for yourself, and trying to blame them for making you feel bad. Did the mean ex-staff force you to watch as they walked out the door with no future? What ungrateful bastards. I can see your noble attitude of self-sacrifice is going to do society no end of good."

Her response?

Her eyes shifted downward. I saw the understanding in her. I was right, and part of her knew it.

"You don't understand." was all she could say.

Still angry, and knowing I had won without a battle, I administered the coup de grâce.

"I hope I never do."

We didn't speak for three days. That was the fight. We didn't talk.

Time passed. Things cooled down a bit and eventually returned to normal, at least until I went all atheist-minded on her. Her response always bothered me though, because when she said I didn't understand, she was wrong. She was the one who didn't understand, but she didn't want to face it. She couldn't.

My wife, my dead wife, wanting children but always somehow miscarrying, fired a woman who was trying to raise a family. I think it bothered her somewhere in a place very close to the surface, and I think her unconscious answer to the dilemma was to fall back on her two religions: cash and the church.

She ended up following the God of Cash. That god always won, which meant her other religion became upset with her.

Our capitalist system works best if employees are constantly available and have no interest other than moving the company forward. When children are thrown into the mix, all sorts of problems are created because parenting forces an employee to split their attentions between the company and their children. Inefficient, and in our culture, unacceptable. Hire someone without kids, without a spouse if possible. Divest yourself of them when any unfortunate spawn assert themselves on their performance.

Naturally the church, Hellen's church, has other ideas. They want their flock to produce as many little followers as possible, for the obvious reason indoctrinating kids is a lot easier than converting adults. It really is like taking candy from a baby. Spiritual candy. Hellen's religious upbringing was against damaging a family in order to maintain a profit margin, so she was trapped by her position. Threatened by it. Normally someone as confident as Hellen would have railed for an hour justifying the firing, but to simply tell me I didn't understand? I could see she wasn't convinced. My having called her on it simply exposed a flaw in her personal morality she didn't care to examine.

The sun is shining and is still too bright. Since they lowered my dose, I find the sun painful in the mornings, especially since I can't really move away. The light moves slowly down the bars of my traction rigging to my brow, causing me to sweat. The jitters I feel in my gut make me short tempered. I press the call button with the hope someone is available to come and close the blinds sometime before nightfall. This whole idea of family is pissing me off. Our cultural attitude towards family, the one we brag about, the one we showcase on every television show and movie, is a giant lie.

We don't want families; we want employees. Children are loud and messy and the ultimate proof of our lack of control over the universe, and we resent everything they need. Resources go to the state, to the company. What right do children have to make demands on them?

Hellen once lobbied to have a playground replaced by a sitting park. She was part of a neighbourhood committee created to build this unspoken child-free zone. It was to celebrate a wealthy deceased couple who had established the first branch of her bank some sixty years earlier. I asked her about it once, and it truly never occurred to her the kids who played there every day would have nowhere to go.

"They'll find a spot somewhere. That old park is run down anyway."

The mothers and fathers who had rested while the kids played somewhere safe were now without a haven.

"It costs a fortune every year to keep that fence maintained," she had said.

The park she and her committee created exists today as they envisioned it, and save for the crickets and the raccoons, it is unused. The land is overgrown with weeds and the benches left unrepaired as they age. The job done, Hellen's committee disbanded soon after the park was built, and none of them will ever have to answer for the land going fallow, or that all of the families who once lived in the neighbourhood have moved on.

Since then, no new families have come to take their place.

A popular outdoor pool nearby was closed three years before they re-purposed the park, with money also being the excuse. They didn't need a committee to shut it down, and in its place today sits a parking lot.

What are we saying to our kids? What are we saying to our future? Are these the priorities of a healthy society?

The sun is directly in my eyes, blinding me, and I'm frustrated and confused. I've been in this bed for something like three weeks, and the person I can thank for it is happily dead. I wish there really was an afterlife ... so I could send her a PFO.

"Thanks for not being a friggin' human being Hellen."

*"I told you before, you brought this on yourself."*

Where the hell is that nurse?

My body hurts. My mind hurts. I can't see.

Fuck.

I'm human. At no point did I ever agree to a situation whereby having a kid would be tantamount to an economic crime. A healthy society remembers its roots. Civilization was created with the sole purpose of making families safer. Raising kids was much more difficult in the days when food sources were unreliable, so our solution was to domesticate plants and animals. We took charge of our food supplies, and from that forward thinking grew a stable society, eventually allowing the prolonged education we take for granted to become possible. Education that allowed our culture to grow technologically. The advancements that followed as the centuries passed allowed more children to reach an age where they could raise their own families. Through our work, we created civilization.

It was only after we invented the gods, and let their earthly representatives run everything, the whole thing started to fall apart.

The gods we made only wanted followers. Families were a side effect, so for thousands of years the gods could bullshit us claiming they loved families, but our latest god is not so cool with that. Money, economics, the immutable rule of the cash god over we, the corporeals. This new god has seen what families are, and it wants nothing to do with them.

A healthy society should place the welfare of families as a priority. Anything less is cultural sickness and an evolutionary dead end.

With the sun still in my eyes, I speak to Hellen. I can see her face in front of me, blurry and judgemental.

"Hellen, do you remember the woman you fired? Do you remember her name? Your god took her family as a sacrifice from you, and you didn't even have the decency to remember her name.

"Did you deserve to die Hellen? Because you were working against the good of the species? I think so. I don't know. You were working against the good of people. We humans want a society that values the future, values our species and its place on this planet, and values our families, whatever their description. You value your God of Cash, your selfish and destructive superstitions, and above everything your tired and relentless desire for things.

"We humans are not impressed."

I'm happy when she doesn't answer.

## JULY 19, LATER THAT MORNING     9

A big guy just walked into my room and turned off the call button. He introduced himself to me, and in my surprise I completely miss his name.

He is working on my IV, checking the flow rate in that bored familiar way nurses have, and watching him work I can't look him in the eye. His heavy fingers manipulate the thin tubing, and I see his hands are hairy and calloused. I wonder if he's washed them recently. I think I'm afraid of him. His greenish-blue nursing uniform doesn't convince me he's really a nurse, and I suspect he might be here to cause trouble.

People do that, don't they? There are people who sneak into hospitals to steal things, to hurt people, while dressed as staff. I know I've heard of it.

"You're looking better today. What was it you needed by the way?" he asks. He looks me in the eyes as he says it.

I'm startled by his familiarity and directness. How would he know I look better?

I motion with my good arm to the window, and reach for my pen and paper. He figures it out before I get to it though, and apologizes for not having thought of it already. I watch through my irrational distrust as the big hairy nurse walks over to the window and closes the blinds. My eyes are immediately grateful, and I notice he doesn't start digging in my drawer.

"My wife can't sleep with the blinds open, even at night. The room needs to be pitch black or she'll be restless and twitchy until morning and I won't hear the end of it. If you want I can pull the curtains, just to make it a bit better on your eyes. How's the pain?"

This torrent of speech surprises me. The other nurses seem to see me as dead weight, held wet and fast on a string. He can apparently see me through my dressings, and because of it I find myself questioning my distrust of him.

I nod my head no, very gently, and as I do I realize he doesn't know which question I'm saying no to. I motion my arm to the blinds and shake my head gently again. I don't need any curtains. I then scrawl on my pad, "Pain. Very bad."

"Gotcha." he says. "You're due in less than an hour. I'll get it ready so you won't have to wait."

I feel better hearing this. I thought it was at least two hours until my next shot.

I haven't been sleeping well since they reduced my dose, and my sense of time is screwed up. I realize I like this new nurse, but I wasn't ready for someone so overtly male. I don't like how the unfamiliar is always so scary.

I know why though. I feel so vulnerable, and thinking about it I feel a new anger well up within me. Hellen put me here, and I wish she were alive so I could rage at her. Instead, I'm tied up inside and out, and I tear my bed apart in my mind. Claustrophobic and alone, I know my whole marriage was a scam. I was her crutch, the man she used who allowed her to feel she still had a right to call herself human. I let her do that to me.

I hate myself for letting it happen.

The big nurse is standing next to my bed, and with the comfort of an old friend he starts the routine. He checks my heart rate, blood pressure and temperature, marking everything down in my ever growing file.

He lifts my good arm to get the pressure cuff around my bicep, and I quickly become aware of the difference between how it feels when a man lifts my arm versus a woman. Because of the accident I'm quite small, but I've always been in good shape, so small for me is still much larger than most women. When a female nurse lifts my arm, unless I'm able to help, it's clear an effort is required. Mr. Big Nurse has no such troubles. My arm doesn't present any challenge to him, and he had no problem getting the cuff on. The contact is different as well, and I find I miss how the female nurses tended to brace my arm against their hips.

His hands are dry and hot. What an odd feeling.

He takes my temperature quickly, and then listens to my breathing with a stethoscope. Heart rate and pressure appear on the machine, and all the various numbers are jotted down. He's good; he knows what he's doing.

"Your heart rate is up, blood pressure too. Probably nothing, but I'll watch it the rest of my shift to make sure you aren't having some sort of reaction to the reduced dose. I should probably let you know, the doctors are thinking about removing the wires from your jaw in a couple of days. Your notepad is going to be obsolete soon." He says the last part with a grin, as if I had accomplished something the doctors didn't want or expect.

I notice he even has hair on his neck, just above the collar. This man is a gorilla, and he is my nurse. It's no wonder I was afraid of him, he looks like a character from some Smithsonian Stone-Age diorama.

I see a sweaty Cro-Magnon male, gnawing the thigh bone of a mastodon. I'm staring at him through thick museum glass, learning about his time from seeing his artificially-dirty, polyester feet. They hold his shiny wooden form upright and noble, beside his hairy and productive, polyester female. Their lives are lived on the fake earth of the museum display, showing us who we used to be. As if to make a point, the plastic tusk of a boar has been knotted into his beard, and that tells us he is very primitive indeed.

His work done, the big nurse leaves the room. I'm once again left alone to tend to the silence. In spite of my smouldering anger at Hellen, I find I feel good, better than I have in a while, and I don't know why. I'm still afraid, feeling more exposed and vulnerable than I ever have in my life, and these are not the sorts of things that would normally make a person feel cheerful.

My red meat brain churns through the blood food it craves trying grasp a wet thought. Smouldering chemical intellect makes itself aware of something it hadn't noticed before, and it sends the realization upwards, through the pale thin layer of emotion, through the crushed layers of meat and viscera, into the conscious parts of me where I spend my life. I realize why I feel so much better.

My giant caveman nurse, he speaks to me as a person, and that means I'm on my way back to being human again.

It never ceases to amaze me how much I've learned from people who have bad BO.

## JULY 20 — 10

The bed is warm, I've just had my shot, and I feel the morphine doing its work. My mind wanders, and the tiny specks of blood from the needles leave such small stains on the sheets.

I see our species. I see it as the beginning and the end. The lens through which all we do is judged.

> *"You've become good at that, haven't you. While the rest of us have seen the light and have chosen to follow the path, you wander off, pointlessly, into blasphemy. Our species as beginning and end? What is that even supposed to mean?"*

"Don't be obtuse, Hellen, it's obvious. Are we hurting ourselves? Are we damaging something our species needs to survive? If so, we are doing wrong."

> *"How very quaint. What if it's a government doing something so heinous it causes people to suffer or die? You atheists have no morality, so what*

*does your 'species as beginning and end' do then?"*

"Others must stop them."

*"Haven't you ever heard of The Rule of Law? No nation would allow its citizens to usurp its power, to tread on its sovereign rights, without intervening. What you are talking about is vigilantism. What you are suggesting is revolution."*

"It doesn't have to be. Nations can chose to do good as easily as not, and they can influence other nations. Even assuming you are right and we are talking about individual action, is that against a law? Is it vigilantism to protect ourselves? Is it a revolution when we merely force an adjustment to our priorities?"

I think of our crimes, and how so many of them are committed in the name of gods. Can the gods survive our judgement? Can the greatest god ever created by us, the God of Cash, survive our need for justice? Will we judge it worthy of our trust?

Floating and calm, I think these dry papery thoughts into the room. What is money anyway, but an artificial limitation on how we use and allocate resources? Money is control. Will we tolerate being controlled forever?

*"Big, heavy ideas, and you with your jaw still wired shut. You would presume to judge God? How arrogant could you possibly be? And let's get another thing straight. Cash isn't a god, it's a means of distributing resources equitably. If it were a god then I would be a polytheist, and that's an extremely offensive thing to imply. God created money for us to use, and we are provided for each according to our needs."*

"Do you really believe that Hellen? Is it really so impossible to see how the monetary system has become god-like?

"So much of our western culture is designed to turn us into

consumable units of production. A litre of gas, a pound of coal, a human resource. There is no compromise, and everywhere I've looked the people are forced to serve their government. But who does the government serve? A person? Maybe a family? In North America we serve a class, but in the end it doesn't really matter because we are harvested like grain. An obscene natural resource - the human resource, and we are put to use until we are used up. Then we are replaced. The God of Cash must be served."

My forehead is sweating, I can feel the moisture on my brow, and I'm floating in my thoughts and angry at Hellen. I hold onto my sheets because they are keeping me level with the universe. My mind keeps up the pace. I can see my ideas standing in front of me explaining themselves, and I try to forget why I'm here. An idea talks to me from my past and I listen.

> "You make it sound like slavery, and yet look at what we have. Look at the wonderful lives we all live! Television and movies show the world just how successful our way of life is, and this bounty has been given to us by God. The Lord rewards his followers."

"Television? Our sit-coms always show happy, well adjusted people in situations that never happen, living lives almost nobody could aspire to, and you want to use that as an example of how good we all have it? That's positively delusional. The poorest characters will invariably own a home, and the average charmingly unemployed person can usually afford to spend a few hundred dollars a day on coffee and clothes. There is no valid connection to the real world in those shows. The people I carried on my bus didn't have sit-com lives. What they live are the hurtful and cruel side-effects of our culture's priorities. How often have I watched as time wore them down, their once joyful hearts ground smooth and hard, the unyielding stone reflection of our mercy."

Hellen liked sit-coms, and of course that was a secret she would never admit. In public she would say sit-coms were for the mouth-breathers. The unwashed masses. In public she was above that, and if she were alive today, I would shame her for her hypocrisy. I would tell her the truth about her illusions regarding our society. I would make her understand.

> "You are truly beyond redemption. Go ahead, tell me about my illusions. Tell me all about my stone cold mercy."

"You can't be serious, Hellen. How can a person compete with that sort of romanticized cultural spam? If everyone is told having a family is simply the greatest thing in the world, but you know all it will get you is nothing but higher taxes, a complete loss of free time, and no reasonable expectation of advancement at work until they leave home, what are you going to think?

"A person faced with that will feel robbed, believing their sub-par life is somehow an exception to the norm. Eventually they will accept it, internalize it, and in such fertile soil feelings of inferiority will sprout, eventually growing into the Stockholm syndrome of our time. Universal and useful."

I pause. Is that where we are? I think so, but it shouldn't be that way.

Looking at our culture, our society, I've tried to find a way out of this death spiral, and it always comes back to the family. That's the important unit, the thing to protect. But we have been taught to believe we don't know better, so we fight our instincts and comply with the wishes of our gods, and the result is our broken, offensive culture.

> "I don't see that. I see people having children before they have established themselves in a career, before even securing full time employment. How can they expect to finish their education, get a good job, by making such

> *poor decisions? God never intended this. Those broken homes are a result of leaving the teachings of the church behind, to wander the desert searching for the salvation they abandoned."*

"I think you're baiting me Hellen. Why can't a family be more than how our churches have defined it? A family is a group of people who work together to better themselves. It's a fluid and dynamic thing, and it includes people from all age groups and all so-called lifestyles. As they evolve, so does society. Parents raise their children, and in doing so they raise our culture. Do you remember when I suggested to you just because two men wanted to adopt and raise a child together, they didn't have to be gay to do it? You were so offended, and I'll admit it was an unusual thought, but who says it couldn't happen? I suppose there could just as easily be a group of straight women who, for whatever reason, might decide they wanted to raise a child together. Why was that such a rebellious thought? If our society places the interests of the family first, then logically, any organization of adults who gather together to raise children should be similarly protected. Even encouraged."

> *"Two wives? Two husbands? Why not six men, an aunt, three grandmothers and a grandfather, all raising little Johnny? You are speaking in barbaric riddles."*

"Do they all want to raise their children to be people who respect our rights as individuals within a species, and its place on this planet? Then why not? I say do it, and have fun."

> *"You will rot in hell for that attitude. You will rot in hell, and all my prayers won't be able to save you."*

Silence.

I don't have kids. I think about that, and I wish I understood better what it means to have someone need you so much, to be so entirely dependent and still love you. When I get out of here, maybe I should look into doing my part to better the species, and learn how to help someone raise their kids. I've lived my whole life for myself, and I feel like I should give something to the future.

That would be healthy.

I rest, my legs pulled tight in front of me, and I understand it's unlikely I'll ever have kids. But I have the descendants of all those born to others, and I think I owe them something. Even my pain in this bed is a gift from my ancestors - those stubborn apes who refused to accept every injury as a death sentence.

I wonder what I can offer the future?

My gorilla nurse has done a number on me. Except for the anger I'm feeling towards Hellen, I feel better than I have in days. I'm still feeling the effects of my reduced dose, it's only been three days after all, but the pain is better, and tomorrow I get the wires out of my jaw. I'm looking forward to the day I can forget my pen and paper.

The morphine dances through my thoughts, my bones think of gravity and my soul of children, and as they all become weary the bed starts to feel warmer. Soon I feel they will sleep.

## 11 JULY 21

My bird is back.

Perched on the branch outside my window, I realize I haven't seen him for a long time. With little else to do I've watched for him, and after all this time I started to worry something might have killed him. My sarcastic side worried he may have been done in by his maladjusted wife. Unable to know for sure, I held to the hope he was just busy, and it seems my faith in the universe has been rewarded.

Here he is. Loud and healthy.

It's hard to believe I could barely hear him when I first arrived. Today his songs are drowning out everything else. The smell of bedpans, the necessary nausea of badly prepared food, the constant calls over the PA, all of it forgotten as he sings. My bird, making wonderful music and celebrating life.

The distracting sounds of nature are welcome, as I get the wires out of my jaw today. The process sounds scary, but they tell me it's quick, and I'm looking forward to a time when I can speak again. This scratching of notes, my primitive pictographs on the walls of this air-conditioned green cave, is getting old, and like my bird friend I want to make some noise. The doctors tell me I won't be able to talk right away. It seems the damage to the muscles of my face was so severe they think I might have trouble. Something to do with the nerves being heavily bruised. I have to admit I don't really know what they meant, but I don't care. Just being able to open my mouth even a fraction of an inch will be one of the greatest freedoms I've experienced since I got here.

I am settled in, anxious to start, and I relax a bit as my bird entertains me with a little dance. The doctors will give me a small dose of pain killer to relax me before we start, and I'm thinking in my current state of mind I could probably skip it. Then I notice the bird's movement. Usually he is so fluid and hypnotic, but somehow it's changed. He seems nervous, jittery. His head darts quickly, left and right, as if he were trying to catch someone standing behind him. His beak dips down, rubbing against the branch, like a chef sharpening a knife. Then he stabs it into a small hole, almost faster than I can follow. I'm guessing he's searching for food. He keeps up this routine as I watch, and then I notice a cat, sitting motionless behind him in the tree.

It's hard to convey the sense of claustrophobic helplessness you get while in traction. I'm a prisoner in my bed, watching a bird, my friend, in immediate mortal danger, and there is nothing I can do about it.

I try to shout my warnings through the wires, my throat raw, my lips wet. The sound is crushed by the pain, and I'm held fast, utterly silenced.

The cat is a typical short-haired tabby, entirely unremarkable in any way that matters, and it's sitting in the crook of a branch about three feet away from my bird. Well within striking distance. My bird friend senses something is wrong.

As I watch, I imagine yelling at my friend to fly away, but I know there is little hope. If he doesn't realize his dangerous situation soon, the cat will take him.

A cheap horror movie, with me strapped to my seat. The actors are real. Blood, speaking the language of injustice and fate.

The cat is obviously fully focused on the bird. It's sitting nearly motionless, whiskers twitching as he stares at the prize. I can see him making minute adjustments to his stance, and it's clear he is planning on making the short leap to my friend for some breakfast.

The bird, my small friend, twitches and hops, his beak rubbing from side-to-side. Unaware of the danger.

A gust of wind slowly rocks the branch, and the cat adjusts his balance to compensate. The cat's movement is subtle, but enough. My friend sees him, the cat knows he's been spotted, and in a desperate effort to complete the hunt, he lunges. The bird is in his element though, and easily takes to the air and disappears. It was barely a contest, he was airborne and gone in a split second. From my bed the action was over quickly, just a bright yellow twitch, and the cat was alone.

The cat is left hanging on the branch by his two front legs, claws out, digging into the bark to keep from falling. I don't know how high up my room is, but I'm guessing the second floor. That puts it at about twenty five feet. Can a cat survive a fall of that distance?

I watch him, angrily. He has righted himself, too easily, and he's trying to figure out what to do. Resigned to his failure, he walks along the large branch towards me. He's relaxed, walking slowly along its thinning path, and as he steps onto the wide stone sill of my window, I'm shocked to see he has decided to watch me. He sits, erect as an

Egyptian idol, surveying the room through the glass. We make eye contact, and I can't help but look away.

I am not impressed.

Alone and tense from this drama, my door is opened and I can listen to the bustle of the ward. I'm more anxious than ever for the procedure to begin. My face still feels swollen, but not nearly as badly as it had been all those weeks ago. Some foolish part of me remains convinced after the wires come out I'll be perfectly capable of asking questions and giving orders.

Nearly unblinking, the cat's gaze follows the team as it begins to filter into my room. A doctor with severely parted hair, wearing a bright red stethoscope that would look more appropriate on a clown, a couple of nurses, and the standard worshipful entourage of interns. My big nurse is among them, and I'm happy to see him. He acknowledges me with a nod, and the doctor describes to the interns what he is planning to do. They listen attentively, eyes crusty and red from lack of sleep, trying hard to be sharp.

Then it begins.

A needle full of Demerol is dispensed into my IV to calm me down. This is the standard practice in the hospital whenever they are about to traumatize someone. Then they pull out the tools: needle nose pliers, wire cutters, some sort of giant hypodermic full of a clear liquid, but without a needle. Lots of gauze. In spite of the drugs that are starting to enter my system, I feel my heart rate rise.

The interns watch as the doctor works, and I feel myself pulled back and forth, being treated to a ride.

It takes them about half an hour to cut and pry the wires off, and I learn the fluid in the hypodermics is to rinse the gruesome accumulation of bacteria and protein shake from my teeth. It tastes terrible, and the pain is quite impressive.

I endure the whole process invisibly, sweating into my bandages and not able to make a sound. My gorilla is assisting the doctor. He looks me in the eye once in a while to see how I'm doing, but doesn't say a word. When it ends I feel like I've been beaten and left in a ditch.

Meanwhile outside, my tabby sphinx remains attentive. I can see his eyes tracking as he follows the movement in the room. He watches as the contents of a needle are emptied into my IV, and I know I'll be feeling an effect very soon. I can see the park is busy with life, and as the effect takes hold, I watch in love as dogs and people stroll together with the birds and the raccoons.

Right away the mattress feels softer, and the rods in my bones seem unimportant and far away. I will the cat to move, to interrupt his stony composure and make him leave, with no success. I'm not too worried. I fall slowly inwards, the drugs make my mind spongy and clean, ready for company, and I look at the mess that is my life and tut-tut my thoughtlessness.

Somebody is going to have to clean up in here.

As I fall asleep, the tabby stares through me into my room, and I stare back at the world through him.

# 12
## JULY 21, EVENING

I can smell metal. It's in my mouth and my nose. I can bite into it, and the tinny feel of it on my tongue makes me wretch.

I'm waking up from the morphine, and I feel like hell.

With effort, I glance towards the window, half expecting to see the cat, but the sun is nearly down, and the cat has gone. My face is sore, from my ears to my neck. It feels hot and loose, like my cheekbones have become smaller.

As I work through this drugged stupor, hearing the familiar noises of hospital routine outside my door, I remember my jaw was undone today. That explains my sore face ... my sore head. This sudden memory doesn't comfort me though, as I realize I'm afraid to open my mouth. The muscles of my jaw become tense, my face wood. Unwilling to test my healing self, I lay stretched in my bed, worrying.

One minute. Two minutes. So much pain these last few weeks, and the hold it has on my will has me petrified by the thought of trying to move. The fear holds me, the room silent, and I can't seem to break free. I imagine if I try to open my jaw, even just a small amount, it will fall off into my lap, leaving on my face a scream that will never end.

I'm quite the poster boy for freedom. Give me even the slightest taste and I clam up, in both the figurative and the literal sense. I need to get over this.

I hear my inner voice, strong and authoritative, telling me to stop this foolishness and act.

"Open your mouth," I tell myself.

My jaw starts to quake, fearful little tremors, as I relax the muscles clamping it shut. Slowly my teeth part, millimetre by millimetre, and the pain is incredible. Soon it stops me. It's too much, I refuse to move anymore.

I reach up with my good hand and touch my lips.

Thick sausages, wet and repulsive, greet my fingers. I feel along the watery numbness for the opening, for the space that should be there, and I find nothing. No space. No gap. My jaw that feels painfully stretched isn't even open wide enough for my fingers to find the opening.

"Don't think about it, don't give up, just keep going," my beautiful strong voice tells me.

I will my jaw to open wider, and I learn what it feels like to punch yourself in the face.

My head is thrown back onto my pillow and my mind is reeling. The room swoons, and I do my best to hold onto consciousness. This pain is different. This is deeper, right in the muscle. In the bone. It feels as if

I'm prying my jaw off of my skull, pulling it down so hard it can't possibly stay attached, and yet my fingers tell me my jaw has barely moved. But deep in the bones of my head I can feel it pulsing, and through my tormented efforts I think to look outside. I need to distract myself from this nightmare.

The park is lit up, trees and grass shining wet in the darkness. I can see a path through the leaves of my branch, and in a small clearing next to the path there is a sculpture I hadn't noticed before. It looks like bronze, and I watch as it glows that warm bronze glow, holding fast against the darkness. The effort to focus is making me forget this horrible mortal war I'm waging with my body.

I forget my jaw, watching the people out for an evening stroll. A couple in love holding hands. A man and his dog, each catching up with the other. No children, probably too late, but teenagers, just a few, travelling in those teenage packs that scare the old folks so much. They look happy and immortal. As they walk, I wonder if they can feel the grass through their shoes the way I used to, and I almost feel it again watching them. Each step sinking into the living grass and holding me up, steady in a bed of nature.

As I watch, the envious voyeur, a part of me starts to work my jaw again. I imagine the cartoons I saw as a child, the wolf characters who would hoot and howl when a woman walked by, stamping their feet and whistling. I visualize opening my mouth like that, and eventually the muscles start to relax.

Slack-jawed and attentive, staring at the pedestrians as they make their way through the night. In the artificial light, the sculpture stands guard over their culture, rooted and solid in the grass. Keeping them safe in the wide darkness, guarding them all from the danger our eyes call night.

My hand reaches up, my lips are sensitive, the new flow of blood is causing them to tingle and sting. I can feel progress, and I find myself trying to fight a painful smile. The hurting is there, deep and impossible to ignore, but I earned my smile, and since it's already here I plan on letting it stay, if only for a minute.

A bead of sweat rolls down my forehead onto my cheek, and I look up again. The lights on the hill are so bright, even through the thick foliage, I can't imagine how I could have missed them before. The sculpture is alone in its isolated pool of light, and I watch its solitude. I watch steadiness, holding itself up and simply being.

I can see the real world from here. I can hear it calling me back, and to help guide me the sculpture sends its beauty into my room. Into me. I feel that love coming back. The desire. The longing. To be somewhere else, to stand up and embrace the things I hold dearest. My bird is alive, and now I have a sculpture, and they live together in the real world.

My jaw opens wider, and my heart looks up and smiles.

The patient slowly closes its mouth to prepare. Its broken limbs looking somehow animated, ready. The eyes are stronger, more hopeful. In charge.

It opens its mouth again, and a rasping croak escapes into the room.

"hel ..."

It tries again, more forcefully, and there can be no doubt, this person is trying to talk. One last time he steadies itself, and looking out the window, broadcasting its will and its love, he lets out a distinct word.

"Hello."

The real world looks in, satisfied, and he smiles back. The pain is showing in his eyes, but nowhere else.

## 13 JULY 22, MORNING

A big surprise today. Apparently I'm ready to have the traction rods removed, which means I will no longer be trapped in this bed, half-suspended. Considering I only had my jaw unwired yesterday, I'm feeling overwhelmed, but happy. I got the news from none other than my new favourite nurse, Markus.

The gorilla has a name.

I was waiting for him when he walked into my room at the start of his shift.

"Hello, what's your name?" I blurted, before he had cleared the door.

It came out as a weak sounding wheeze, but the words were distinct, and I got the effect I was looking for. He replied with a grin.

"It's Markus. Good morning!"

I wasn't expecting him to understand me so easily, and as I processed this new information he did the routine. Blood pressure, pulse, bed pan and small talk.

"I hear they are planning on taking out your rods. You are on your way to being bipedal again."

"Will it hurt?" I rasped.

"No, not really. They dose you up before they start, like they did yesterday, and then finish with the morphine. I'm told it feels weird, but not painful. One good thing, it only takes about fifteen minutes to finish."

I was surprised by that. The thought I could have rods going through my bones was hard enough to deal with, but the idea they can get them out in just a few minutes? I don't know how that's supposed to make me feel.

My pain is bad this morning, and I'm more than relieved to see Markus arrive with my morning shot. But before he does, I want to ask a question. My face and jaw hurt quite a bit from my efforts to speak, so I stop him with a motion of my arm, then with his attention I motion to the window.

"Sculpture?"

He looks at the window, and it's clear he's never stopped to look out. I watch as his eyes focus on the distance and I can see the dawning of understanding as he realizes I can see a sculpture in the park on the hill.

"Can you ... name?" I croak. My jaw hurts like hell.

"You want to know its name?"

I nod my head. My whole face is throbbing, and I really don't want to say anything else.

"I can take a quick walk on my coffee break to find out. OK?"

I nod again.

He lifts the blanket, and I feel that familiar jab. Its effects aren't as overpowering as they were when I first arrived, but they still slow me down a lot. I feel the familiar chemical comfort spread through me, so profound and artificial.

Introspection, even this plastic version they sell in dark alleys to madmen, is something I've never had time for. Until now.

I am on my knees and I pray to my god, keeper of the chemical bond. Oh carbon, oh hydrogen, make my mind the gooey blob of happy love you always do.

Outwardly I giggle, and Markus glances back as he hears it.

I see him crack a smile at me as he leaves, and I notice something else. Markus understands. There has always been something about him I couldn't place, and that look told me what it was. Markus was an addict.

Markus used to be a worshipper of the chemical bond, and the look in his eyes makes me suspect he understands the power of these drugs as much as I do.

I close my eyes and swim in the hallways of this church of blood, and as the morphine makes me smarter and smarter I see him growing smaller, smiling at me from the past. He is sitting like a Buddha, a skinny scarecrow Buddha in a dark room, and he is eating from a tray. I walk up behind his haloed form as he sits. Touching his shoulder with my hand makes him look up, and as he turns his head to look at me I see his mouth is full of hypodermic needles and pills. I watch horrified as he chews, crushing the needles as they pierce his cheeks, swallowing them down. His hand reaches up to rest on mine. I step back, utterly repulsed by the sight of him ... by the sight of his eyes, so dark and hollow. I'm terrified of him, terrified of this skeleton of Markus who is killing himself in front of me. I try to pull my hand away, but our hands are merged, blended one into the other, and I can see we are meant to die this way. He will kill himself, and I'll go with him.

I yell "Markus! Please! You're going to kill us! Markus!"

His eyes, grey and black and dead, look up into mine and change. I'm petrified as our eyes lock. My heart, my soul, my past and my future, locked to this dead shell of Markus.

His eyes see me and they understand.

Panicking, I'm forced to watch as his dark and corrupted pupils begin to shrink, the irises change, taking on colour. Flecks of blue and green spread and glow. I can see them as they become animated, become the eyes of a human being. Eyes with emotions. I can see the caring, the love of others I could always sense from him before. It's back, and I can see the rest of him morph as I stare, his skin smooth and glowing, flush with blood. Muscles, atrophied and weak, take on their more familiar form and the health that made him so real exists again. I'm still connected to him, our hands tied together in blood and skin understanding. I look down, confused, as I feel the strength start to flow through his hand into mine, making my skin feel warmer, making my bones feel eager to move. I'm bathed in his glowing life, and I close my eyes. I breathe.

"I am so sorry. You're going to need me soon, and I almost forgot to get ready." The words come from the universe, from my mouth, from my past and his.

I open my eyes and I think I'm back. Outside of the window I can see a pale day, clouds are keeping the sun from having too much fun, and through the branches I can see my sculpture. I watch it while taking shallow breaths. The dreams I've been having since I arrived here have an intensity I'm still not accustomed to, and this one was no different. I breathe as the dream works its way through my waking self, and I start to believe I'm awake, that reality is back.

On the hill I see my sculpture, a guardian of our future. The clouds seem surreal and I enjoy the sight of them. They part slowly, to reveal a small slice of sunlight that completes the scene. The piece is brightly lit, the grey gloom pierced by yellow and orange, a halo around reality that lets me leave my bed and watch in awe.

A figure approaches. It pauses before the bronze, penitent, dwarfed, then bends at the hip in supplication. After a moment of contemplation it rises. I watch the most beautiful sight I've ever seen.

I close my eyes. Calm, peaceful, I allow a quiet sleep to overtake me. I am nature. My bird is nature. My sculpture is nature. We are all worthy of worship.

I understand.

## 14 JULY 22, AFTERNOON

I wake up and the light feels subdued. The ward is quiet, and I'm feeling pretty good about my little epiphany. When trapped in a hostile world, there seems to be no better escape than the profundity of chemical nirvana.

Is this how my father saw reality? Every thought awash in only the deepest and most meaningful hues? I can see the attraction, but it's artificial. Only a lens. I can feel that. Nothing I see here is any more vivid or truthful than what I see out there in the real world. This place is going to be holding me down for a while longer though, so for now this lens will have to be enough.

I flex my jaw as I think, is this how Hellen saw her church? Her cash?

That thought never occurred to me before. The idea her skewed views on the world were made somehow more real to her based on the vantage points given to her by her gods.

*"My Gods? Plural? You keep saying that, but there is only one God. I think your obsession with my beliefs has made you an offensive little man."*

"The truth is always offensive to people who don't want to hear it. Face it Hellen, you worshipped two gods. Your Bronze Age God and your God of Cash."

Is that how she could reconcile the moral incongruities, the vast intellectual differences between her separate religions? Were they somehow the real world to her? More real? Were things like the outdoors, nature, the stars and our planet, and all of the people and animals that inhabit them, were they all just figments, ghosts, ciphers, made real only in the context provided to her by her gods?

I think so.

If that's true, then her death makes more sense. Our conversations weren't about ideas, or my beliefs compared to hers, they were about worlds. About universes. I was tearing the walls of her church down, erasing the digits of her moral bank account.

How can a person live without their world? How can they live if the world they spend a lifetime building ceases to exist? I called her beliefs superstition and greed, she called them ego and id. I said she was deceiving herself and her super-ego agreed.

Why couldn't she see that? Why couldn't she see how her clinging to such anachronistic attitudes was killing her? But I've answered my own question, haven't I?

She couldn't see it, because for her there was nothing to see.

I thought I could bring her to my world and talk her into joining my rationality. I really believed somehow she would be able to see it. Instead, I tormented her with incomprehensible vernacular. Words and ideas that didn't make sense in her world, the world of her two gods. I thought she had tried so hard to understand she eventually broke her mind, but I know the truth. She simply saw herself as cornered, and she hated me for it.

I take a deep breath and try to feel sorry for her.

I am nature. My tides and my meteors, my gravity and my earthquakes, are without meaning or purpose. I am and I do. There is no understanding what I am, or why.

There is no why, there simply is.

I'm not getting any comfort in that line of thought. I spoke of rationality, and in my ignorance created insanity from it. I'm laying in bed healing slowly from the wounds she inflicted on me, and I take no comfort in the fact I never meant to kill my wife.

But of course I did. As surely as I'm here, shattered, in this bed, I wanted her dead. I wanted her Gods to die, and from the ashes of her lost churches, her lost Gods and their icons and coins, I wanted her to rise for me. New and clean, the vessel of nature reborn. The beautiful habit of life, the birth and the rebirth, affirmed in her new self.

Why couldn't she see all I wanted was to destroy everything she ever was, for her to be something else, something different, something I saw as greater, something that in so many ways her church and her cash didn't even believe existed?

She was taught nature didn't exist, and I wanted her to become a part of it.

My jaw aches from this thinking, this tense understanding. I'm looking into a chasm and I can't see the bottom. I can't keep blaming myself for what she did, and yet here I am, doing it, and doing it well.

The day is still grey. The light seems to be slower, my room less ventilated. I'm laying in bed wishing I could talk to Hellen again, the futility of explanation my beguiling opiate. Knowing what will happen, I quickly stretch my newly liberated jaw as wide as it will go and the pain throws me deeper into myself. Into the mood of the day.

My glorious morning, my visions of the beauty of self, of nature, are gone.

## 15 JULY 23, MORNING

Waking up, my neck is sore. I've found being forced to stay on my back all night has the effect of making my head do all of the tossing and turning. I'll be glad when I can do the impossible and turn in my sleep once again.

The light is brighter today, and looking outside I know yesterday I was right. Everything we do, everything we make, is nature. My bird is nature, I am nature, and so is my sculpture.

Especially my sculpture.

Stuck to the side of my table is a yellow sticky note, at my eye level. On it is written;

Henry Moore. 'Bronze Form.'

I see Markus was able to get out long enough to check the name of the sculpture for me. Was that him I saw yesterday? Such a meaningless mystery, and the idea cheers me up a bit. I don't know who Henry Moore is, but the name of the sculpture seems confident enough. Bronze Form. That explains the way it glows in the morning light. Warmth that seems to come from nowhere.

I'm thirsty and a bit anxious for breakfast. I notice as my condition improves, I'm hungrier. My mom would be happy, she loved it when I ate a lot. She was such a fighter against the raging maternal stereotype, and yet when she was painted with the 'mommy brush,' she looked the part.

This morning light is making it hard to guess the time. Judging by the sun's elevation on the wall it must still be early. How much time will I have to spend staring into the abyss of my bored and confused self, as I wait impatiently for breakfast?

Hellen would never have understood my little epiphany. To view everything as nature, especially the works of our species, would have seemed trite to her, even a kind of blasphemy. She saw the work of mankind and the world of water on stone as separate and distinct. Certainly not something that could be classified together in such an all-inclusive folder.

For her, it was God and money that built bridges, and cars, and buildings and monuments. To her, these churches, these monuments, these comforting ideologies created by her Gods, were living proof of mankind's ascendancy over nature. Its eminence. Nature was the rutting goat, the blighted crop, the locusts and the plague. The beauty of nature resided solely in it scenery, in its more colourful and exotic animals, and even then beauty wasn't attributed to wind or water or evolution or gravity or rocks or stars, it was sold to her as something God did. Something God did in a day, and I can't remember which one.

I said something like that to her once and it upset her. There I stood, smug, my world looking over my shoulder, not even thinking it possible she couldn't understand me.

Is there such a thing as a self-evident truth? Probably not, even in my world.

My thoughts are interrupted by my door opening - in walks my doctor. I know it's him because he's wearing his dark hair severely parted at the side, and he has that familiar red stethoscope. The white jacket, the absence of any real interaction with me, my doctor.

He asks the nurse if I've been prepped, have I had my 'wee little dose' of relaxation yet? And then notices she didn't follow him into the room.

Definitely my doctor.

Without acknowledging me, he puts a cordless drill down roughly on my table. The sudden weight of it pushes the table a few inches further over my bed. Now I have a great view of my yellow sticky note, and of a large drill. A metallic green sticker on its side tells me I can expect the power of 14.4 volts.

Electric drill goodness, right here in the room with me, on my table, over my bed, and I was hoping for some eggs. I can see this is going to be an unusual day.

Outside of the room I can hear talking. I can't make out the words, but plans are being made. In a minute the nurse, a woman who I recognize from her braided blonde hair, says a quick hello and let's me know they will be removing my rods soon. She says it in a way that makes me think of a flight attendant. She is so artificially happy about it, and I can see she isn't even in the same room with me, at least as far as being in the moment goes.

She would be a good human resources person.

As she explains the details of what I'll be going through the next few days she injects a drug into my IV.

"Just a little shot of something to relax you," she says.

"... so I can be operated on while I'm awake?" I add.

I know this routine and I find myself waiting for the feeling, the coming of the pleasure foam thoughts. I wish I could get this done without being so artificially befuddled.

Drugs in the IV take a bit more time to hit me. I don't know why, but they tend to feel slower. I'm already getting the first hint of the easy-bake calm that's to come, but I know it will be sneaking up on me for a while yet. I watch as the nurse with the braids leaves, and in spite of the massive doses of morphine I've survived, doses that would usually put an end to this sort of thing, I involuntarily have my first sexual thought since I arrived.

I notice her ass.

See what I mean? It just sneaks up on you.

I try to pull my thoughts away from these fantasies of her, but my lizard brain imagination has been engaged, and all that floats around in my drug-addled mind are pictures of her and I, our hands on each other. I can see the look of lust in her eyes as she grabs my shoulders and draws me to her.

The doctor returns, goal-oriented and confident, and I am very much aware I'm sporting a fully erect penis.

I am the teenage boy and the doctor just walked in on me. Will he notice my discomfort? I feel my cheeks flush, the colour spreading hot and shameful across my face, as I hope 'it' will go away before he notices. Privacy does not exist for those who live within these walls, and I feel very little hope I'll get out of this without a major humiliation. Naturally, the stress of this situation is making the odds of my rebellious organ deciding to withdraw from active duty slim to none, and I can see the sheet above my groin shaped in that all-too-familiar tent, just waiting to be discovered.

I don't care about the rods they are going to remove from my legs, I don't care I can feel the drugs having their way with my chemical state. All I want is for my libido to get itself under control, for the evidence to recede in time for some sort of dignified escape.

Markus walks into the room carrying a large tray wrapped in a green cloth, and this is getting bad. I don't want him to be the one to find my little surprise. He places the tray on my bedside table, then, with a comfortable speed born of practice, he starts taking it apart, preparing the contents for what's to come. It looks to be full of sterile instruments and gauze pads, and obviously he is in charge of assisting the doctor. So far so good I think, and I take some comfort in the fact at least the female nurse who started this little hormonal cascade isn't here. That would just about end any hope I have left of subduing this earthy beast.

Meanwhile, in the southern regions, the locals are agitated. Tensions are high, and I can sense if something isn't done soon, there will be trouble. I'm so hard it hurts.

The brochure didn't mention anything about this.

Then it happens. Without warning Markus turns to me and lifts my sheet, probably to start removing the sterile gauze that surrounds each rod as it exits my body. His eyes refocus as he looks down and I know he sees it, there can be no doubt. There I am, naked and as big as life. I try in my mind to find the words to describe my abject horror to him, but he doesn't even flinch, and before I manage to open my mouth to speak, I find myself thankful and relieved as he simply puts the sheet back down and resumes shuffling instruments. A moment later he leans in towards my head and asks in as subtle a voice as his great size can manage.

"Did you want help with that?"

I'm lost. My humiliation is absolute. What can I say? This giant hairy man is asking me if I want help with my raging tumescence, my inappropriately wooden friend. Am I supposed to be relieved? What the hell could he possibly do?

All dignity gone, I'm resigned to this utter and complete failure to control myself. I look at him, defeated and small, and I nod my head yes.

Apparently, my problem is about to be in his hands.

Then it happens. That tray of equipment Markus had been preparing is knocked off my table, landing right on my chest.

Small gauze pads, short measured pieces of tape, and all sorts of other non-life threatening medical bits land all over my upper body. Meanwhile the tray arcs right over me and lands roughly on the floor, making an astonishingly loud clatter. They will have heard it in the next ward, and everyone stops what they're doing to help get the process back on track.

I can see what he is doing. Distract me from the my problem in the hope buddy down there will go away. It's not going to work. My whole body is dedicated to maintaining this hardness, and it will not abandon its efforts for some spilled gauze. Then Markus leans in again.

"Sorry about this."

I am about to nod my head, maybe try to mutter something to make him feel better about his failure, when a hand reaches into my chest and crushes my heart.

Markus, reaching across me as if to gather gauze, deliberately jostles the traction wires holding my injured arm. Just the smallest very calculated nudge from his elbow and I can't think from the pain. The shock of it holds me rock steady, my whole body tight and defensive. He hit me just below the rod near my shoulder, the one closest to the big bones in my core, and I can feel it tearing through me, over me, as the pain washes itself across my consciousness, slowly finding its equilibrium.

The pain killer in my drip wasn't ready for this, and in spite of whatever relief it's providing, I'm at the mercy of my body and its reactions.

I look up, my eyes watering as the waves pass over me, and I see the room is not in any sort of disarray. The small mess had been cleaned within a few seconds of the tray falling and a new sterile tray has already taken its place. The smell of chemistry and medical intent is heavy in the room, and a foot away from me my doctor is talking to Markus.

I'm invisible.

As I fight the urge to clench my jaw, my doctor finishes his conversation with Markus and together they approach my bed. Without any hesitation or concern my sheet is lifted, and Markus looks me in the eye and smiles. Mission accomplished he seems to say.

I'm sweating and sore, and I really hope the next time I get an erection of that magnitude it doesn't end as badly as that one.

The room is busy with people, interns mostly, and I'm really curious how they are going to use that drill.

A nurse begins to unhook my arm and legs from the weights, explaining to me what she is doing as she lowers each cable before removing it. One after the other, my limbs rest on the bed for the first time. The feeling of gravity is not comfortable to say the least and I can feel the blood settling into new and painful locations. It's almost more than I can take, this new weight on my still grotesque-looking limbs.

Trying hard to relax, I find myself performing a mental head-to-toe self-examination. The process is always the same: head, neck, shoulders, etc, etc, all the way down. What I find is troubling. I'm weak, so weak my legs are somehow too heavy to move, and both are sore from what feels like blood pressure. They feel as if all of the blood in my body is flowing downwards, making them feel larger, stretched, like water balloons ready to burst. My fractured hand is feeling it too, like my fingers are being squeezed fat with blood, but for some reason my arm isn't affected. At least, not in the same way. The painful swelling is there, but very much subdued. Instead I can feel an ominous sharp sort of tightness running all the way up my arm and into my shoulder. As I think about what it means, I worry the tightness will begin to reach deeper into my chest, and I start to wonder if I'm not having a heart attack.

Wouldn't that be funny. Survive the accident and die from a heart attack a month later.

Laying here, trapped by gravity, I can see the doctor reaching for a large silver tool I hadn't noticed. Bolt cutters?

I can't watch this, and I close my eyes. Then I feel it, in my legs first, as my whole body is being moved by the efforts of my doctor. Snip, thump. Snip, thump. Snip, thump, clang. One after another he cuts the ends off of the rods in my arm and legs, straining against the hard metal, and the sound I hear is the rod snapping and falling to the mattress and the floor.

Apparently he is only cutting off one side of the rod. This is a weird experience.

I open my eyes to see what's going on and Markus says to me he will be cleaning the little nubs of steel sticking out of my limbs. He says he needs them sterile so they won't give me an infection. I'm just the drugged and exhausted patient, so in spite of not having a clue what he is talking about, I don't argue. From my lips the single word 'cool' is heard as he applies the blood red Betadine.

Then it hits me. I realize how the rods are coming out. I can't believe I didn't think of it before. The rods are threaded, like screws. The doctor is going to put one end in the drill, and then he is going to use the drill to unscrew them from my limbs.

The realization is making me ill just thinking about it, and the doctor confirms my guess by stating exactly what I just surmised. He says it only takes a minute or two each, and after that I'll be free from the traction for good. That last bit he says with his own version of the happy airline attendant smile.

I think I'm going to be sick.

I close my eyes and allow the drugs to calm me down. My heart rate is up and the pressure in my legs is making me think of a balloon being filled with water again. They feel like they're going to pop, and as I fight the panic and the pain, I can feel the doctor working down there, trying to secure the drill to a rod. Secure it to me.

Done, the chuck tightened and ready, I'm attached to a drill. I feel like a weekend project in the back yard.

Then it starts. The familiar electric whine very low and slow. I can feel the bolt turning in me, starting with a jolt as it breaks free of it's position, then the slow grinding spin as it exits. There isn't really any way to describe how it feels, a warm threaded friction turning inside me is not an easy thing to explain.

It's a very uncomfortable sensation.

The first rod comes out, and the doctor moves on to the next. Then the next.

And the next.

Then it's done.

The holes the rods left in my skin are small, almost not worth noticing. I've cut myself worse slicing tomatoes for dinner. Markus puts a couple stitches in each one, and that's it.

I'm no longer in traction.

I lay in bed, for the first time since I arrived here, and I try to get a sense of myself. Everything is out of place, and it feels like nothing is going to work ever again. I sink into my hospital mattress more deeply than I like, once again feeling trapped. Markus moves my little dresser next to my bed and then leaves with the doctor, and I'm alone with the random staff who remain from the procedure. One of them lifts my blanket, and before I know what's hit me, a needle plunges into my ass, and again the veil of morphine begins its decent. Drugs in the muscle take effect very quickly, and in no time at all I'm dreaming about all of the reasons God and I wouldn't get along.

## 16 JULY 23, EVENING

"We are not the stewards of nature, we are its creation." That was the thought on my lips as I woke up from the morphine.

My newly liberated body is on the bed, floating on the last legs of a morphine haze under a thin hospital blanket. I'm free of everything holding me down, save for my broken frame. My body is the weak link, and any sort of true freedom I can imagine is impossible until that link is strengthened.

I have a lot of work to do.

I'm not sure why I woke up saying that. It's true I've been thinking about a lot lately and much of it does come down to nature, eventually. What nature is, our role as a species within its framework, and I guess part of me wants a reminder of my place in it.

I haven't eaten today, nothing since yesterday evening actually, and in spite of my second morphine hangover in as many days, I'm hungry. I haven't seen anyone in the room since I woke up so I press the call button and hope for the best. To my surprise someone arrives within a minute.

"Anything to eat?" I mumble. My speech must be improving because the nurse understands immediately.

"We've saved a tray for you. I'll get it," she responds.

I don't know what time it is, so I hope it's only a short while after supper. The idea of cold mashed potatoes with a side of warm melting gelatin is not doing much for my unexpected appetite.

"We are not the stewards, we are its creation," I repeat to myself. The idea is certainly at odds with Hellen's convictions, at least as far as her two religions were concerned. It makes me think of a picture I remember from my childhood, hung alone on the wall in a busy corridor of my grade school. It portrayed Jesus looking meek and solemn, kneeling in the woods surrounded by smiling woodland creatures. Its meaning seemed clear to me even then. We were above the animals and we were meant to be their keepers ... at least that's what I got from it. If that wasn't the primary meaning then it was certainly implied, and even at such a young age, I found the picture disturbing.

I was a funny kid.

I found it especially odd animals would worship someone who was probably going to eat them. It seemed masochistic to me, even though I had no idea of the word back then. It made me think religion had no idea what nature was. To be fair, at that age I didn't either, but what I did know, from the frogs and crayfish in the stream behind our yard, from the birds nesting in the trees near my school, and the dozens of little bat bodies I found frozen below the eves of our house sometimes, was the picture was wrong. A complete fiction.

A few decades older and I'm an adult. All those years of life experience should have allowed me to figure it out, right? The thing all the religious scholars and all the creepy pictures like that one, seemingly missed.

The answer to 'What is nature?'

Well, amazingly enough, I do have an answer.

It's simple.

Nature does not exist.

Nature is an anthropomorphism. Nature is just another god we've created to explain something obvious. There is no such a thing as nature, any more than there is such a thing as money, or time. They are creations which we find convenient, but in the greater scheme of things, they are meaningless.

So how are we its creations?

That's easy too. Nature, as I understand it, is simply the random events of matter and space, extended through time to such an extent we cannot possibly imagine the results. Working from that, the meaning of our eventual evolution and our current status as the most prolific of the apes, as well as the most destructive, is clear.

We are simply one possible outcome of leaving matter to stew for a few billion years.

Thought of this way, things like pollution and global warming really have no meaning for nature as nothing we do could ever hope to hurt it. How can you hurt something that doesn't exist anywhere but in our collective imagination? Think about it. Plutonium is just as much nature as is a baby seal, and each has as much right to exist as the other, whatever that's supposed to mean. They are not inherently good or evil, they just are. Now if you prefer baby seals to plutonium, and someone adds plutonium to a baby seal, then perhaps you will see plutonium as evil, but that's just your personal viewpoint.

That's just your opinion.

In a hundred-thousand years, both the seal and the plutonium will have changed so much any debate over what was good or bad would be pointless. It would be the intellectual equivalent of debating the intelligence of Cleopatra having worn a red dress to breakfast one random morning.

So what does that mean for us as a species? Well, we are a creation of nature in the sense we have been derived from the random events of matter that led to us. We are a result. From that, to the assumption we're somehow the stewards of something as elemental as time or matter, or the things they create together as this galaxy ages, illuminates an arrogance on our part which is beyond belief. Seen that way, what matters to us as a species becomes pretty clear. Although we aren't the stewards of nature, our actions within this environment can harm us. Therefore, we should be vigilant of our actions, not because we might hurt nature, (we can't hurt a system composed of our projected moralities) but because we can hurt ourselves.

Assuming evil does exist, how would it be defined in this context? How does pollution or habitat destruction or global warming become evil?

It becomes an evil when placed against the good of our species.

Seems like pretty obvious stuff when you think about it.

My tray arrives and I feel my rib cage stretch painfully as the bed is raised for me to eat. I'm not used to this amount of mobility, and this sudden reminder of my healing ribs catches me off guard. Apparently this new freedom is bringing with it new pains.

Feeling a bit short of breath, I start to eat.

My good arm brings small portions of jello or potatoes to my mouth, and gingerly, I chew them down. I try the carrots, soft and cold, and they actually taste really good. I finish them off before anything else. The fact I'm able to sit up and feed myself, as opposed to being hand fed while strung up like some sick medical ornament, is having a positive effect on me. In spite of the new pains in my arm and legs, I feel slightly better. Life goes on.

At least it's starting to feel like it might.

The evening wears on, and as the sun goes down I ask the nurse to leave the blinds open again. I want to relax my thoughts with my sculpture. We play together in the evening light, talking of stars and galaxies and time. I talk of my telescope at home, and of the arid plains and soaring mountain ranges of our moon I've observed through it.

Like good wine, good company is relaxing, and very soon I fall asleep for the first time without restraints.

# 17 JULY 31

I feel melancholy, and through my window I can see dark clouds in the distance. The view doesn't show me much: the park, the hill, my sculpture and the people who mill around it. The weather - rain one day, sunny the next, is always a surprise. I adjust myself in my bed for the thousandth time today and look out. My vision has become an end unto itself.

It can get pretty boring, laying in bed all day.

I've become accustomed to not having the rods in me, although the freedom of movement took longer to get used to than I would have guessed. It shocks me how I adapted to them so quickly. I don't really remember doing it either, I just woke up to the visual assault of seeing steel rods running through me and life went on. In hindsight I would have thought it would have caused me more emotional upset than it did. Instead, I spent three minutes examining their work, and the next three weeks surfing the endless morphine wave.

I think I was so amazed I woke up, it made everything else tolerable.

The holes where the rods used to be healed up quickly, and they don't look like they'll leave much of a scar. The same can't be said of my hip. The part of the scar I can see, straining against myself to do it, is still angry looking. In a twisted way, it looks like the glove box never left.

Considering what happened, I guess I should be happy to be here at all.

Using a small hand mirror the nurse left for me, I can see my face is looking good. Just a bit of blue and black around the eyes, but they tell me no permanent damage was done, so I'm happy. The few little cuts that show are not doing anything scary, and I already think they add a certain amount of character. I was never unique in terms of my body, always relatively hairless and clean, so this will be a new thing for me.

"Hi there, you can call me the scar guy."

Did I mention laying in bed is boring?

The doctor tells me they will be getting me started on a physical therapy program soon. I'm not really looking forward to it. I'm still in a lot of pain, and the idea of getting out of bed and trying to walk just seems insane. The doctor also says I should be using a hand exerciser to try and get some tone back in my bad arm. So far, I can hardly do more than keep it resting on my chest, anything else is uncomfortable. I can wiggle my fingers though, so I'm hoping maybe the discomfort will pass quickly.

Aside from those looming clouds, it's a nice day and the park is busy with people. I'm seeing a lot of dogs lately, and it is makes me think I might want to get a dog as well. Franklin would love that, I know, but I think having someone to go for walks with would be nice.

I've been doing so much thinking since I arrived here, and I'm a bit intimidated by it. I came out as an atheist so long ago, but I was married to a religious woman and her social circle really didn't respect that sort of thing. What was I trying to accomplish? I wore it on my sleeve like a badge, a spiritual challenge. I paraded it around the way a hunter puts deer antlers on the hood of his truck. Why? What was my point? I don't think I was trying to impress anyone, but thinking about it, I probably looked as if I was.

I was the guy who was always sitting on the fence, and when I finally chose a side, nobody cared.

But that's not the entire truth.

If Hellen were still alive, her anger would tell me she cared, and I wouldn't be trying to figure out humanity in my head. I would be busy pointing out flaws in her religion, in her church, in how our culture worships cash, and how cash is manipulated to hurt us. If you had told me (in those days) I was hurting her, I would have laughed at you for a long time. Hellen? Hurt by me? Not a chance. Her faith in her two religions was rock solid, and all I was doing was trying to bring her over to an even better faith, one based on the truth ... as I saw it.

Me, standing on my mote of dust, yelling my truth into the universe at her. Believing she could hear me as I spoke a language she could never hope to understand.

I was an arrogant and cruel bastard, I think.

Am I different? I don't know. I realize trying to make her understand would be futile, so perhaps my constantly engaging her in that thrust and parry of beliefs would end. What would it accomplish?

There was so much my world had to teach her though, and she could have been so much happier here. She could have been so much more than a token, so much more than another pretty pawn of men. She loathed those sweaty little self-appointed gods, whose only desire was to be worshipped. In my world, gender is meaningless, at least as far the intellect goes.

Ideas are transient but plumbing is forever, right?

All those conflicts she suffered. Her gods, church and economics, warring for supremacy within her; she trying to reconcile them, to find a peace she could trust. Her soul was the living field of battle, her actions and thoughts were the prizes to be won. All of it would have been gone. So much of her life would have been better if she could just have seen my view. Seen the world the way I did.

She would have seen our current attitudes were not a culture, not a society, but a sickness. Our self-destructive love of cash? A sickness. Our need for gods and churches? More sickness. A mental disease we as a species need to rid ourselves of at all costs.

I'm a bastard.

I told my wife her worlds didn't exist and she listened. I told her to trust in them was insanity and she was angered. I told her she would have to abandon her old worlds to live in the splendour of mine, and she knew a terrible little part of herself believed me.

That terrible little part abandoned her past. It abandoned her sanity, just as I said she should. It made her question her comfortable worlds, just as I told her to do.

She lost her mind, and with nothing but faith left, she killed herself.

I can see the sky is clouding over. I lived, she died, and who was the better person? Did the right person die?

A heaviness continues to fill the sky, showering my sculpture with rain. I'm not hungry, my appetite is lost, and having been right makes me feel no better. My arrogant and vain ideologies have managed to do nothing more than kill, as people of so many cultures have been doing for thousands of years.

I watch the rain fall, my view through the glass obscured by water, and I ask myself again.

Did the right person die?

I hate myself for it, but the answer is on my lips as the rain sends me to a troubled sleep.

Yes.

## 18
### JULY 31, NIGHT

I am floating in space.

I'm dreaming.

This is something I've been doing a lot lately, these awake dreams, these lucid dreams. I'm floating in the void of space and looking down on the earth. The globe is beautiful. The shape is the most perfect sphere I've ever seen. It defies logic. The clouds are skimming along the surface, nearly touching, and the effect is magical. Vast white banks floating over land and sea, immune to gravity, just the velvet fog keeping everything warm.

From my vantage point the land is a dark liquid-green, the earth crinkled and rough, the vast oceans reflecting flecked sunlight back into space. Looking down I see the blue cast of water, deep and forever.

We live on a wonderful little thing, this earth, and I keep my thoughts away from what's to come.

The flashes of light are so small they hardly register as more than lightning at first, but their numbers grow, and the light doesn't fade like the sudden crackle of thunder. The light stays, slow and mean, and it's spreading.

I'm dreaming but I can't close my eyes. This new view is mine to loathe as I see what's in store, what's just around the bend. I look ever more closely until I can see myself and Hellen laughing and sharing beer in a cafe. We don't see the lights, the biblical glow coming for us in our pleasant afternoon stupor. I'm even closer, floating in space and yet also sitting with the couple. I'm the idea they both share between them, and in the distance I can see it coming, hot and red, fast and total. The world is melting in its path.

They sip their beer and joke about a politician.

The wall is coming faster, it's almost there, and they still don't see it. I look in Hellen's eyes and I try to communicate to her she should run, I'm not safe to be around, I caused this. She can't hear me, I'm not really there. I'm in a dream, she is dead, and we can't speak anymore.

They talk to each other so calmly, and I watch the last seconds go by, inevitable and solid. I look at my other self and I don't want to speak. I know he brought this on them, on this perfect little world, and I hate him. I can't speak for my anger, my spine wrenching painfully trying to contain it. A human's wrath unsafe to release and shameful in its violence.

I sit at the table, at the cafe at the end of the world, sipping my beer and joking about a politician with my soon-to-be-dead wife. I joke, and then putting my beer down I look right into my own eyes, my beer-drinking self looking at me, my dream self, and he says: "Don't worry, you live."

They are swept away.

I watch myself tossed into the maelstrom with Hellen and the world, our bodies destroyed by the flying debris, burning in the shattered remains of the city, and he is looking back at me.

He is smiling.

I don't wake up. I try.

I am pulled back up, back into space, and I can see the destroyed cafe, and the blighted city, and the continent and then the globe. Our perfect globe. It's no longer called earth, because anyone who knew it by that name is gone. From space it glows gently, so beautiful and sinister in the darkness, the lights of the cities extinguished, replaced by broad sweeping fires.

They glow, they spread, and then they fade. Embers become ash.

Our planet remains - the continents are alive, the oceans and clouds unchanged. Such a deep blue. The mountains are there, the deserts are there.

And the green is there.

The cold ash nourishes the land, once again uniformly green. The red anger has passed, is still passing, and the world still breathes. I am so high I can't see the life I know is there, but I can feel each of the plants and animals as they roam their new planet, the days unremarked by anything but the seeds. Iron is rusted. Concrete has crumbled. Buildings built to last decades - gone in a day.

The vast ocean of life on this perfect globe is unimpressed, and the only loss I feel is a sense we might have been better had we known. The feeling passes as I begin to understand how we did know, and in spite of that knowledge we still chose to do nothing.

I'm floating in space and my old home is shrinking from me, the distance between us growing. Our former planet is not mine any longer, and I feel I've lost the right to spy on its new life. I fall further and further into the void, and as I do, I can see a new intelligence being formed. New ways of reasoning. Our scraps and our leaving are sometimes dangerous to them, and those areas are left alone, the taboo places where fools once roamed. We are not even legends, we are nothing but mysterious examples of tool use and construction.

So much of what we were rests deep in the mud under the ocean, washed out to sea in a thousand eons of rain and wind. It will remain there until it is recycled, deep in the heart of a dying star.

I'm falling ever further away, and from my great distance I can see a man and a woman sitting and drinking in a cafe on my former earth, forever in the future. The man looks up into my eyes, so deep in space and time, and he smiles.

He knows he will live as well.

## AUGUST 4 — 19

I can't eat.

I'm not hungry, and I can't stand the smell of the food they have been bringing me. My dreams are haunting me, and I'm finding myself more and more loathe to rest. My body is slowly healing, and I hate myself every time I find an old skill has returned.

I can use both of my hands to place a straw in a cup, and I wish I wanted to drink.

I dream about Hellen. I dream about this planet and our species. I dream we are ants in a colony and we are waging war. We are waging ant war as the farmer pours gas into our little ant hole. We all die, the ants fighting each other in death, not even knowing what killed them.

Markus looks more and more concerned when he visits. He is working on the ward next to mine, so his visits are infrequent, but I can count on him dropping by, usually every other day. Yesterday, he said he would send someone to talk to me - a counsellor to help me work through this. As he spoke, my thoughts were focused solely on how I would keep the psych staff out of my head.

What the hell right did I have to live? Was I a productive person? I drove a bus. I could have done more but I chose not to. Was I lazy?

I'm not finding any solace in my park or the people who inhabit it for a few minutes each day. My sculpture has nothing to say to me anymore. They are so far away, in a world I barely recognize, and I can't imagine how I could ever fit in with those people ever again. I'm the outsider. The murderer who cannot ever rejoin the race.

I'm the plague the prophets warned Hellen about. I'm not economically viable.

My pain meds have been reduced again, and as much as I wish they wouldn't, I can see why they are doing it. I'm getting better. I'm still a long way away from walking, or the impossible dream of returning to work somehow, but I'm not the broken animal brought in with a stretcher and a bucket.

Now it's my mind that's broken.

I am not hungry.

The room is so dull, the paint so uniformly dreary, I just want to close my eyes to it. All day long just stare at the inside of my eyelids. I would, but for my sleep. I would close my eyes but I'm afraid of my fucking dreams.

Hellen. She's been silent for a while. Why?

So religious. So in love with her jewels and her cars and her houses and her job and her church. So in love with her friends who were all as equally pious as herself. So many cars and houses and cash. So many gods.

I used to think she was a good person, even when she was destroying the species through her actions. Through her ideologies and her rhetoric. She was evil, and yet she was a good person.

I'm so judgemental. So tired. I just want to sleep.

I return to my senses and see someone has left food for me. I've been receiving glucose drips for a few days, so I won't starve, not soon anyway, but this is a surprise. Someone has left me a box of macaroni and cheese.

Uncooked. Just the box.

Is this some sort of joke?

I reach up and grab the box, with the intent of putting it into the trash next to my bed, but the familiar heft of it, the sound it makes when I shake it, they transport me back to my youth.

I can't bear the thought of throwing it away just yet.

I place the box under my pillow, and I'm silent. No motion. Just me and my noisy wet organs, living in the guilty room Hellen has built for me.

Time passes, and I've been made into the perverse voyeur, silently observing the world outside live its life. The park has changed. The fall is coming and the longer grass is going to seed. It's looking a bit weary. The trees haven't fully turned, but they too are showing hints of the autumn to come, and my sculpture is vigilant - the steady witness of this passage.

Together we watch the universe age.

I haven't heard from Hellen in weeks. I'm afraid.

## AUGUST 8 — 20

Why am I here?

That should be easy, I'll just run down to the library and check out something written by a Greek.

Maybe Plato.

Seriously, I need to know. Without a purpose, what am I? In this hospital I'm nothing, and can I lay claim to anything more when I leave? I'm a walking digestive tract, without purpose but to fill my gut. What does that make me?

I'm so tired, I should really stop torturing myself with this crap.

I haven't been able to eat for a week, and the counsellors are bargaining with me. The doctors don't care, not really, as I have a drip. They feed me sugar water and vitamins, and I suppose it might be years before I die, and not from starvation, but instead from the watery fat of the glucose drip.

They will leave me alone to work this out as long as they have a direct line to my chemistry. If I were to do something rash though, like tear it out, tear out their line into my heart, watch how fast I would find my broken self tied back up again.

Even here, we are made to remember our place.

I've noticed Markus is still the only person who can see me. I exist for the rest of them, but Markus can see me, and I suspect that's why he is worried. I dreamt of him again - a horrific dream where I ate him. He was asking me to do it, and I wasn't even squeamish, I just dug in. That dream ended badly, with me looking into my own eyes, through the eyes of the nearly-consumed Markus. I could see the lust to devour him reflected back at me, the lack of shame. Mindless.

I was not afraid of Markus' consumed skeleton. I was afraid of myself.

That animal mind, the dirty part of the brain that will eat a slug when it's hungry, it was looking into the eyes of Markus and it couldn't see him. Not at all. It just saw food.

I looked into myself and I didn't like what I saw.

I see all the wars. I see all of the prejudices. I see the racism and the bigotry. It's all there in me. Right there on the surface and I can't hide it and I don't even care to try. It's just there and I show it to anyone who asks.

What happened to all that love I was feeling? I loved the world when I woke up, and now I would just as happily bury it all in the sand.

I adjust myself in the bed, and with my good arm I raise the head just a bit. The doctor says I should start walking to the bathroom soon, and to do that I'll need to become vertical again.

Being more upright makes me dizzy, and the sense of pressure in my legs is overwhelming.

Our species has managed to kill more of its own than any other, of that I have no doubt. We are geniuses at applying intellect towards the destruction of our bodies. I'm living proof. I didn't even need a weapon, just a few months of time to turn a sane lunatic into an insane one. What can be done to save a species who can kill simply with a thought?

The gods must be crazy? Not a chance. We are.

We kill everything. We do it for fun. For profit. Out of ignorance or just to impress one another. If we could travel to other worlds we would kill everything there too.

All the aliens we see in the movies, the ones who come to our planet to kill us? They are simply us, projecting our evil selves onto the universe. The fact we manage to kill the aliens is us trying to make our subconscious feel better ... and sell tickets.

If we arrived on a planet, and the locals weren't our technical betters, we would eat their hearts and, if we could, breed with their women. We'd wear their ears on chains around our necks, and pridefully send home photos of our conquests, so our loved ones could see just how much good we were doing.

We've done it before, countless times.

Our species has been so perfectly corrupted by religion, by cash - I don't think we should be saved. For the good of the planet, we should go. Let the suffering stop, and allow the planet to resume its work existing.

Happily existing without us.

I'm not hungry. My muscles have atrophied to the point where I look like a charity ad, the kind that tries to get you to send money. To give them cash so the fat people on TV can give the unfortunate skinny people food and bibles. The psyche staff have been so nice to me, so understanding, and as our conversations meandered through the territories they'd laid before me, the destination soon became clear. They have a goal for me. A modern salvation. Clean and ordered.

Antiseptic and inoffensive.

I need a friend, and what do they offer me? The same as all the others.

The missionary, come to save you from your culture and your life. Take this all of you and eat of it. This is your new culture, and all of your women will have blue-eyed babies next year.

I'm so small and so alone. I used to watch the news before I arrived here. This world isn't kind to people who don't tow the theological line. How am I going to face the world knowing what I know? Knowing if we don't stop our worshipful deceits we will destroy ourselves.

How can I face them when I know the universe won't even care?

I keep doing this. I torture myself. I spin the ideas around in my head and then stare blankly out of my window, exhausted, and watch the sky darken on the hill. One of the bulbs illuminating the sculpture has burnt out. It's been a week and nobody has fixed it.

Entropy.

My body is getting better. My limbs are healing, but I can feel my heart growing older by the minute. I wonder if I want to get out of here alive.

## 21 AUGUST 13

I had my first physical therapy session today, and anyone who has faced the righteous anger of the physical therapist will know I did not have a good morning. I would have preferred having a limb amputated than deal with that.

They hoisted me upright, and for the first time since the accident I put some weight on my shattered limbs.

It didn't go well.

Sitting on the edge of the bed, the pain was more than I could bear. I was begging it to stop, crying, my spirit broken, long before my feet touched the floor. It was humiliating to be so helpless and in so much pain. Meanwhile the physio girl was goading me on as if I was some sort of weight lifter trying to heft that extra five pounds.

"Just a bit more! That's it! You can do it!" and as she speaks I'm wetting my pants, wanting to die.

My legs inflated like balloons as they were lowered, and as the hands lifted and turned my body on the gurney, I knew all of my blood, my guts, my bones and tendons, they were all going to come rushing out of me through my feet. The pain was more than I ever thought possible, and I shudder just thinking about it.

Safely back in my room, sweating from the memory, I can't help but curse the way everything about pain is always so relative. This morning was the worst torment I can remember ever having experienced, and yet I clearly remember saying the same thing about the pain of being crushed and punctured in the accident, and of my dressings being changed after they have partially healed into my wounds ... and now, I say the same thing about Hellen.

After the session, I was given a big shot of morphine, of course, but it doesn't put me to sleep the way it used to. I've been awake since the session in the gym this morning. Awake, shaken, and brooding.

I'm eating, and in a bureaucratic sense I can see it's making the staff happy. In all honesty, I feel like I'm only eating out of fear and selfishness. I could see the damage I was doing to myself. Staying awake for more than a few minutes was getting difficult, and when I did manage to stay awake I was hearing weird noises, far off voices. Apparently a forgotten part of me exists that didn't want me to damage myself. I don't know if it means anything as I still find myself unable to bear the thought of leaving this place and joining the real world.

The world of humans.

Laying in my bed, surrounded by the smell of me, I feel below everyone else, viewing them from the dirt. From a place below. Through grass and twigs, I watch my betters live the lives they deserve, while I live this rancid little life I deserve.

"You are so full of shit," echoes off the sterile hospital walls.

A chill grips me, when I hear myself voice my obvious self-contempt. I didn't mean to speak. That wasn't me. I couldn't have been me. I'm not crazy.

I hold myself still. I settle my thoughts.

I silently repeat the words, and the stars begin to align against me ...

"You are so full of shit." ... They have judged me ...

"What are you? What indeed! Let me tell you what you are. A selfish, weeping bastard! Do you really think you matter? Like this? Do you really think you are important enough to warrant such a childish little tantrum? Prove it! Grow up! Stop feeling so damn sorry for yourself and fix this shit. Fix your life while you still have one! Get yourself the hell out of this fucking place before you can't ever leave!"

... and the sentence is delivered.

My torrent filled the room, reaching out into the hall, easily louder than the normal afternoon commotion on the ward. The patient next door would have heard it for sure, and in spite of my blurry speech, I can't imagine he didn't understand what I said. He probably thinks I'm having a fight in here. Some sort of psychotic episode.

He would be right.

This is tearing me up. I know where this shameful anger is coming from, but I don't want to face it. I can't go back out there. The world is horrible, people are cruel and evil and I won't stand a chance. I hate myself for thinking it, but I know it's true. I don't want to leave this place, and my body is betraying me by getting well. I'm healing, and I don't want to.

I'm trapped in my bed, countless miles to the floors and the walls, and all I can think is I wish I had a relative. A friend. I wish I had anyone at all. Someone to call. Someone to stay with. Anyone. I'm alone, and not just here. Alone in this city. Alone in this world. I'm alone in the universe - its only occupant. All the evils I fear are simply those random acts of matter moving themselves from one state to another, and I'm afraid of them.

I don't understand and I need room to breathe.

I notice the jitters in my body are gone. Adrenaline is a powerful thing, but its effects can't fight through the morphine fog.

I need to find myself again.

I said as much before when I joked about calling myself the scar guy. I'm not the same as I was before, and is that obvious fact perhaps why I'm so negative? I was so happy to exist when I woke up all those weeks ago, and yet, now, I would happily toss myself off the roof.

Part of me thinks this doesn't make sense, but the honest part of me, the thinking part, knows the truth. It makes perfect sense because when I first woke up I couldn't understand myself anymore, and all this time as my body has been healing, I've been learning a new language. My new language. Before Hellen died I couldn't talk to her because she was in a different world than me, and her final act of revenge was to destroy my old world and put me here. It has made my words, my language, my old self, incomprehensible.

I am changing, I have changed, and I understand.

So much pointless thought, but is it helping me? I'm always tired, always drugged, and I'm always scared. The slightest pain makes me flinch, makes me whimper and cry, defeated. I'm the beaten dog of bed 4b.

Meanwhile, Hellen is standing in the corner of my room, silent. I can see she wants to speak, but she's unable to bring herself to do it.

I think she's afraid.

Time is my enemy, as I heal slowly in my room.

## AUGUST 19 — 22

An odd thing. I don't remember waking up today. One moment I was dreaming of life, the universe, everything, and the next I was looking out of bleary eyes, my dream now reality. I don't remember the transition. Even now, I feel like I'm asleep. The texture of my thoughts are still the dream, and it's disconcerting as hell.

The world outside my window isn't helping.

The sun rose behind a heavy fog, and in spite of my blinds being open, I can't see a thing. The park, the hill, my sculpture, they are all obscured. The view looks two dimensional and grey. A window-sized picture of claustrophobic angst on my wall.

With my damaged hand, I carefully lift a paper cup to my lips and drink. The water is quickly lost deep inside with the rest of me, and I can see I will not be in this hospital for too much longer. I can't walk yet, and the damage done to my insides has been causing me some trouble lately, but if I'm here for another month I'll be surprised.

I think too much here, and I've come to the conclusion the world outside, the real world, is not the same as the one in my head.

My inner world is populated with evil, angry people. Nothing but dangerous opportunists who will do whatever they want to whoever they please, as long as it benefits them. Governments lie to us and steal from us. Gangsters and religious fanatics who inflict meaningless death on us. None of them worried because they know their crimes are unpunishable. The beauty isn't there. I see nothing but the vile and the dirty, and I think that's why I'm so afraid to leave this bed.

I need to see the beauty again. I need to find the beauty in the world.

For the longest time, my sculpture in the park was my beauty, but that isn't enough anymore. It's an inspired piece, but the random acts of nature, man made or not, don't seem to be enough for me. I need to see something more. Something that makes me remember we humans are not as repugnant as I imagine.

I need to wipe the mud and entrails off of our great accomplishments and see them for what they were. What they still are today.

Why do I think humans are so bad? What is it that's revolting me? Our actions? I lived happily in that world my whole life, and it never caused me as much pain as it does now that I'm no longer a part of it. Why is the world I've constructed in my mind so dangerous, when I know the real world isn't?

I don't know.

In an effort to drag myself back from these dark thoughts, I look around my sterile room. I listen to the sounds from the hall. The morning routine is progressing more quietly today. The nurses are subdued, the doctors quieter and less intimidating. I ate my solitary breakfast in a dreamy, soupy, stupor as my thoughts churned in the bleakest corner of my mind. The fog does that I guess. Dulls the senses and the intellect. Makes everyone seem quiet.

The effect of the fog is amazing when I think about it. It's impossible to miss, once you see it.

Coming to work in a cocoon, the hospital staff arrive quietly, deeper inside of themselves. I'm sure they must feel it consciously, just a bit, in response to the world hiding itself away. The lack of clear vision means everyone is looking inside themselves, and from that, their surface becomes more still.

I know about fog. I've lived in a fog of morphine and pain for weeks. I thought I could see through it, but I think it's obvious I can't. I'm not seeing anything but my fears. I'm remembering the ghouls and the ghosts who haunt the human condition, and the lack of clarity is making me see them as the real world's sole inhabitants. They've become the world. I see just the parts I'm afraid of because this damnable fog keeps everything else from me. A fog that keeps me from understanding Hellen and her choice to do us in, rather than deal with the loss of her husband.

I can feel myself wince as I think, because I know that's why she did it. She knew she had lost me. I showed her my world, and she could see I was in love with it, but she couldn't follow me. Even if she could have understood me, even if she had wanted to, she couldn't follow me.

Thinking of myself as I was, I didn't kill her, at least I don't think so. I hurt her, obviously, but not in a way that would destroy her. My having found my own little atheist world wasn't enough.

She was destroyed because she tried to bring me to a place where she could understand me, and I refused to notice the effort. I didn't kill her, I left her.

I was so proud to have figured out she couldn't understand me, living in her different world. I forgot ignorance worked both ways.

At this point, in my world of blood and bandages, that makes as much sense as anything else. Our rough debates, the rhetorical battles fought between glasses of wine and expensive sex, they were only rough because we were both trying so hard to make the other understand. The only reason I didn't feel the same pain she did was because I thought I had nothing to lose.

Two people, already so different, simply grew further apart.

I take a breath while I think of that, and the ache of my healing ribs grounds me. It doesn't explain it all, but it explains enough for me. For now.

Meanwhile, as I try to reason my way out of madness, the apparition of Hellen stands vigil in the corner. I don't know what she wants, but I can't help but feel she is waiting for a chance to strike. Since her return, I've noticed her appearance has changed. Whatever fear of me she may have harboured now seems tempered by rage.

The next time I see my doctor I'm going to ask him to stop giving me pain killers. I need to wake up from this dream.

# 23 AUGUST 21

The paint on the walls of my room looks old. The colour has been muted by age and sweat, and it offers nothing to the soul for nourishment. However, in spite of this bleakness I've found some relief, and it has made things clearer to me.

It came to me last night. Hellen's figure had left me, finally, but the lingering sense of her presence made me anxious. I couldn't sleep. I asked the nurse to leave the blinds open, and in the darkness I watched my sculpture.

Long after the sun had set, the darkness nearly absolute, a young couple appeared. Enjoying the eternal scenery of the night sky, they were looking for a place to be alone. They settled in the pool of light next to the bronze, and eventually they began to kiss. Slow, passionate kisses with the stars and the solitude protecting them as they enjoyed their love.

I couldn't look away.

My heart was tied in knots, I wanted so badly for them to be happy. When they eventually left, I was renewed. I had watched two people, alone in the evening, perhaps alone in the world, fight off the darkness that had oppressed me. They did it without a thought, creating such beauty even I, from my great distance, was able to enrich myself from it.

And then I realized why. I've been seeing nothing but the evil in the world, my crushing emotional burden making everything seem shallow and dirty, but the good? The good I knew had to be out there? I was immune from its influence ... until tonight. Initially I was confused by them. This couple was the opposite of evil, that was clear, but I didn't think of them as good. It seemed thinking so would be doing their love the greatest disservice. I did not see them as good, I saw them as beautiful.

The epiphany?

The opposite of evil isn't good. It's beauty.

I wait for my lunch to arrive and I know I've had that word on the brain for a while. For days I've been trying to figure out why, and now I understand. I needed to find the beauty in the human race, not just because I want to be consoled, but also because it balances the evils I've been seeing. It gives me the stability I need to keep going. Good just wasn't enough, it had to be beauty.

I fell asleep. My normal midnight call for pain meds didn't happen. The night nurse didn't wake me as she did her rounds. For the first time I slept through the night, and I was eventually awakened the next morning by the voice of my doctor, asking what I had wanted to speak to him about. My vocal cords still rough, I made my request.

"The drugs. I want to stop. Can you stop giving me morphine?"

He gave me an odd look, a mixture of surprise and confusion, and adjusting his stethoscope, he said, "No. Not yet. Once you can stand we'll talk, but until then it's too soon. You stop now you'll screw up your physical therapy."

My frustration must have been obvious to him as he quickly added, "Don't worry. Now that I know you want off I can help get you there sooner. Just get yourself on your feet. I want to see you upright."

I was disappointed, but at least I have a goal.

After lunch I'm scheduled for another session of physio, and with this new motivation I'm hoping I can do better than last time. Looking at myself, my hopes aren't high. I remember back to the days before the accident, and although I wasn't any sort of Adonis, I wasn't the mess I am today. My bad arm is healing but it's weak, really weak, and it's not all that useful yet. After only a few seconds of effort, my fingers start to feel like feathers on the end of a stick. Not even much good for pushing stuff around. My legs are not much better. They were both crushed, which means the bones needed plates and traction, but they tell me I was lucky. My joints did not suffer too much damage. My ankles, knees and hips all managed to escape with relatively minor injury.

I will grow old and die never understanding the doctor's use of the word 'lucky.'

With so little injury to the joints, they say I'll be mobile again sooner than would otherwise have been expected. For the first time in weeks, I feel good. My mind at least somewhat settled. I think having a goal is making a difference. I want off the pain killers, and the fact my doctor thinks I can do it has given me something to hold on to.

With my body unavailable to me for so long, my thoughts have taken on a life of their own. Good or bad, my moods have come alive, seeming larger than before. An unexpected adaptation, but considering my current circumstance I won't question it. I'm just glad the future seems promising again. Brighter. This bout with my negative side feels like it's lifting. I really hope so, as I need to move on, and I think I can finally see the path that will make that possible.

Lunch is late, and it occurs to me I haven't seen Markus in a while. I wanted to ask him if the box of macaroni and cheese was his idea. It's still under my pillow, and I suspect it's helped me get through this. I ate my own weight of this stuff every year as a kid, and having something from my childhood, even something as impersonal as a box of noodles, is comforting. I can't explain why I kept it, and the looks the nurses give me each time they change my bedding has had me averting my eyes to avoid explaining myself. But the sound it makes when I shake it brings back memories of boiling water and childish energy. I would have felt like I was giving away Franklin.

"You are beauty, my poor lonely friend. I wonder how you are doing?" I send the thought to Franklin, and for some reason that makes me smile.

Franklin takes nothing from me I'm not willing to give, and in return he gives me his friendship. I've thought of him a few times lately, and I'm guessing it's because I'm thinking of returning home.

I miss him.

Going home. That big deal I wish I didn't have to face. I'm intimidated by the idea of being alone, of needing help and not having it, of having to face the universe by myself. The idea I can simply fall back into my old life and things will somehow be the same is nuts, but that's my vision.

"The fool returned home with no unexpected difficulties, and after a brief adjustment to his new condition, life continued exactly as it did before," I mutter in my best British safari voice. I know it's absurd, and yet still I imagine a week will be enough to get back to normal. I hope the fool in me is right.

It amazes me how I adapt. I was so low, my vision blurred by my contempt for life. Yet in spite of the darkness inside, the hopelessness that permeated me, I'm clearly through something. No debates either, it's just done. I've found my beauty, and that is giving my life a meaning it lacked before. Knowing this, perhaps my doctor was right. I do feel lucky.

I've had friends, both at work and from school, who have battled real depression their whole lives.

Of course, the less foolish side of me knows when I go home I'll need to deal with my body. Dressing. Eating. Bathing. It won't be easy. But I think the thing I'm even more afraid of is dealing with Hellen. I was unconscious during her funeral services, nearly dead myself actually, and I know her death still isn't real to me. I'll need to deal with that. She hasn't been willing to leave me, in this place where death is just work.

We were living separately when she died, so at least I'll be spared having to go through her personal effects. That would have been a tough thing to do. Each object, each paper, every scrap of her life I touched, would have become a divine proof of our love, and the damning evidence of its tragic loss.

I don't know how other families deal with it. Having to sort through such raw proof of one's mortality.

It occurs to me her family hasn't sent a lawyer to discuss the matters of her estate, and that tells me they would prefer to do the job themselves. Wealthy families oftentimes have secrets. I know Hellen's did, and because of that, they like to keep things tight to the chest. It was an ingrained reflex everyone in her family shared. I remember watching them dispatch lawyers to discuss such menial affairs as the size of a photograph in an annual report.

Not sending a lawyer to talk to me about Hellen's affairs is them on war footings.

"I know what they are doing, Hellen. They are keeping your God's relics from me. The cash, the credit, the reputation it granted you. They don't want the family pieces of cross to fall into my infidel hands."

I speak this aloud into the room and I don't know why. I get a chill.

Whatever happens, I'm not really all that worried. Living with almost no expenses for so many years, my paychecks were essentially just numbers deposited into an account I never touched. If I'm careful, I'll have enough money to keep me solvent for the rest of my life, and if I end up not being able to go back to the same work, I'll find something else.

I hadn't thought about that much. Driving a bus can be tough work on the body. Will I be up for it? Looking down at my scars, at my still disfigured limbs, something tells me I won't be.

Oh well.

Lunch still hasn't arrived, and I tighten my arms and legs while I wait. Gently squeeze until it hurts, then slowly release. I'm trying to regain control of my muscles so when the girl in physio asks me to do something I'll be able to find the muscle to do it. It's a humiliating thing, her asking me to do these simple motions, and me responding with nothing but tears. As I worked, I could feel the sweat coming out of me - my hospital smell making me even more self conscious of my failures. Finding the right muscles seemed impossible. They were so weak, when I tried to tense them nothing happened. Even now it feels like I've lost them, lost the sense of them, and until I find them again I won't be able to make any progress.

Flex, relax. Flex, hold, relax.

The pain is still pretty bad, but I can see how my body is improving, healing. I'm better than before, but I still have a long way to go.

I'm trying to ignore the tightness in my gut. My stomach, abused and ignored, is speaking. I'm hungry, and I think that's the first time I've encountered my hunger so plainly since I arrived here so long ago. Another sign of things to come, that unwilling independence, and I wonder once again about lunch.

I think of my nighttime lovers. Pushing back the aggression of this existence to enjoy each other so completely. They didn't see things in terms of the old gods. The God of Cash held no authority over them as they kissed.

Looking for a distraction from my biological self, I think of how my lovers fit in my newly-arranged world. If I can't have food, I'll occupy myself in other ways. My mind wanders over the possibilities and the clock spins its hands. I see time pass, and as it does, I decide things are different for us, the genders of humanity, than they were long ago. Even in my lifetime things are no longer the same, and the realization hurts a bit when I see the implications.

As I worry my way through these little traumas, I find it odd how a person can have an idea, a viewpoint, and how it can take on such a sense of being set in stone, the possibility of change difficult to consider. Give it a small push though, and the view that once seemed carved in granite becomes fluid, shifting and merging with other ideas, eventually changing into something 'other.' Something new.

That's how I feel. The whole time I've been here, bleeding, healing and crying, I've been feeling myself shift. My view of reality is from a different shore now, and it feels correct to me. As if these thoughts had been running through my mind my whole life.

Thinking about what I used to believe, my old self would not have understood.

Family as the centre of civilization? I may have agreed in principle, but no doubt if I was placed in a situation where my actions needed to reflect this stance, I would have flinched.

I wouldn't now. I won't.

> *"You're a sanctimonious ass, aren't you! As if anything you've been going on about makes even the slightest difference to anyone. We don't even have children. It certainly won't be very hard for you to maintain this moral high ground when the test that proves your worth can never come."*

She's back. I can see her standing in the corner, clearer than before. She's wearing a bright red scarf I bought her for Christmas years ago. Her manifestations are really frightening me, and my skin crawls as I respond.

"Hellen, when we were together we had no family. It was just us. We made sure our needs were met and everything was wonderful, right? But, as we enjoyed our perfect life, did we do anything to help those who do have families? No, we didn't, and that's where I've changed. I feel I have a responsibility to my descendants, one which I cannot simply shrug off when it becomes inconvenient. As the world shrinks and our technologies make us much closer roommates in our planet-sized biosphere, the behaviours and attitudes humans could once get away with are causing crisis, and this hurts everything around us. The system in which we were bred, the one that sustains us, will change at some fundamental level and we will perish. The system itself though, this personification of the biological web we are a part of, will live on. I would prefer we live on as well."

> *"You do make it sound so simple. Am I to understand families should be exempt from working for a living, exempt from having to contribute? I hope that's not what you're suggesting. The world is built on productivity, and if we can't count on an effort from every member of society, we won't last. The economy will crash and we will join the ranks of the failed nation states."*

As she speaks, I can see her hands twisting, pulling at her clothes. She is fighting to keep control of herself, and her Christmas scarf is becoming tattered.

"I'm not saying we need to make life a free ride for families, but I do think we can make their lives better. What good is humanity to the God of Cash if by worshipping it, we die? What good are we for the species if we accept being punished for the crime of procreating? I think if the God of Cash has an Achilles heel, that's it. Without new worshippers, without growth, the cult, our economic religion, dies.

"Think about it seriously for a minute Hellen, it's so fundamental to what I'm trying to say. The good of the species requires an environment that nurtures the mated pair. One that protects the family unit, in whatever form it takes. Your wilful ignorance doesn't change the fact you and your bankster friends don't seem to understand how much you need us. Does your God of Cash know how much he needs us?"

As I say the words, I wonder; do we really want the leaders of that one-dimensional cult of the coin to figure it out? I'm beginning to suspect these thoughts, these ideas and this vision, are a curse. An important, life-altering, curse.

As Hellen stands, silent and frustrated, she starts to pull at her hair violently. It comes out in patches, falling from her clawed hands onto the floor at her feet. Then she tears at her jacket and her shirt - the once manicured nails easily ripping the seams. The expensive stitching is no match for her anger. As I watch, horrified, her clothes are reduced to rags, and then, as her hands finally fall to her side, her skin becomes dark and grey. Her eyes sink into her skull, the crucifix around her neck becomes black and cancerous, and I know I don't want to see this.

She is going to scream, and when she does it will kill me.

I'm saved from my frightening vision by Markus. He is in a hurry, taking long steps into my small room, and he's wearing a smile. I'm heartily glad to see him, so thankful for the interruption. Anything to break the spell Hellen's ghost has over me. As I smile my hello to him, I realize the entire time I was talking to Hellen, my muscles were knotted from the tension. I'm exhausted, and my bed is soaked from the effort.

As he does the heart rate, blood pressure and temperature routine, he picks up on it right away.

"You're sweating. Something wrong?" he asks.

"I'm trying to get my legs and arm to work by flexing them, and I guess I didn't see the effect it was having on me. I'm good to go."

It's a lie. I can't tell him about Hellen. About my nightmare standing in the corner. I'm trying to control my breathing, but the vision is still too fresh. She's standing just a few feet away from him.

"Good thinking," he replies, "I'll be taking you to physio today and the doctor says from now on you are to be transported in a chair, not the bed. You going to be OK with that?"

"Probably not, but let's go." I answer. Anything to leave this room.

As I'm lifted painfully into the waiting chair, I try to make small talk. The pain isn't as bad as it was the other day, and talking helps me get my mind off of the panic Hellen is causing in me.

"Have you got that box of noodles?" he asks me, "You're going to need them today."

"That was you?"

I get his big grin as response.

He finishes placing me in the chair and then hands me the box of noodles. I hold them in my lap, my nearly transparent hospital gown letting me feel its cardboard edges easily, and I try to take comfort in the familiar rattle. What a foolish and brilliant thing. I've bonded to this box like a pet, and I'm sure that was what Markus intended.

The hospital air is cool and dry, and I can feel it flow over my stale skin. It feels good, and I find myself fighting an urge to hang my tongue out of my mouth like a dog. The breeze makes me feel unwashed, the oily stagnation of laying in bed thick and imporous, and if I had my way I would be soaking in a bath right now.

"When we get back, if I'm not nearly dead from exhaustion or morphine, would it be possible to have a bath?" I ask.

"You're scheduled for a dressing change, but if physio goes well we should be able to arrange it."

Then we are through the door, leaving my bed and Hellen behind.

I'm already in a lot of pain from sitting, so as we make our way to the gym, I keep working to relax myself. I visualize sitting on the grass next to my sculpture. Looking up, I admire the deep blue sky, and imagine the smell of the air. The scent of leaves and soil.

When we finally arrive I'm sitting in my park, talking to the bronze about eternity and women.

# 24
## AUGUST 21, NIGHT

I'm home.

The room is dimly lit, and looking more closely I can see it's my bedroom. At least it used to be. It's the bedroom Hellen and I shared until our separation, and she and I are sitting on our bed. We're having a glass of wine, waiting.

Hellen is pregnant, and we're waiting for our baby to arrive.

The room is just as I remember it - opulent and wonderful. The drapes are a thick blue velvet, very tasteful, and our big four poster bed looks grand, elevated in the center of the room. Hellen is supported by satin pillows. She liked to read books this way, and I wonder why she is wearing her wedding dress. Shouldn't she be wearing something more appropriate for having a child?

I see her stomach, and it's flat.

Hellen pours me another glass of wine from an expensive looking magnum. I take a long drink, and I can feel the effect of the alcohol. Hellen looks into my eyes; she is so deeply in love, and I worry I'm too drunk to return the sentiment. For a woman about to give birth she doesn't seem to be in any sort of pain. She's quite happy, and I watch her sip wine elegantly from her glass. I can see she is a little drunk as well.

Peering at her through the indirect lighting, Hellen doesn't look like she is in labour, and I ask if she thinks she will have the baby soon. She laughs at me and tells me I'm silly.

"Babies don't come from me," she says, "they come from God."

In a spiritual sense, I suppose she's right, at least for the people who are into that sort of thing, but I'm thinking about the baby.

"Where is the baby?" I ask.

Without any preamble, I lift her wedding dress and look between her legs. As I do this intimate thing, she seems indifferent. With two fingers I move her panties to one side, to see if something is going on. What I see takes a moment to register, and when I finally understand, I recoil as if bitten by a snake.

I don't see anything. No labia, no vagina, no hint of reproductive organs at all. Nothing.

Keeping my voice calm, I ask her about it.

Hellen looks at me sideways.

"I am not that kind of girl," is all I get from her. She is clearly insulted. Meanwhile I'm still holding her panties open with two fingers, paralyzed by the horror of my discovery, and I wonder how the baby will arrive.

There is a knock on the door, and I look up from between Hellen's legs to see her boss standing at the foot of the bed.

Hellen and I don't say a word. Hellen is so exited she is vibrating.

Her boss clears his throat, and in a deep and resonate tone he says: "Congratulations! For your many years of service, I am granting you both this gift. May it serve you well."

From his pocket he pulls out a key. Without looking, he casually tosses it onto the bed and turns to leave.

Hellen can contain herself no longer. Looking at me with wide eyes she yells: "Is it a boy or a girl?"

I don't understand what she means. The key sits on the bed between us, but she is not picking it up. She asks again, this time more urgently. I don't know what to do. I'm so confused. I reach out and grasp the key. A short golden fob has the only markings I can make out, and I examine it more closely.

On it are two stick figures. A man and a woman.

"Both," I say.

Hellen is overjoyed.

I turn over the mysterious amulet. I'm confused and I need more information. Where is our baby? Why does Hellen have no reproductive organs?

On the back I see a word. A powerful word, making this key a strong talisman of her cash god.

In raised golden letters, I can clearly read the word 'EXECUTIVE.'

# AUGUST 23    25

I'm in a lot of pain. A LOT of pain. Physio did not go as well as I'd hoped.

I arrived in the gym ready for torture and struggle, and instead the therapist told me today would not be a good day to proceed. She never used those words though, not exactly. Instead, she inferred them by sending me back to my room and back to my bed. I suppose she might have used those words, if I had been awake to hear them. I was having a hard time hearing anything, after falling out of my chair and knocking myself out.

Today I learned I'm motivated. I am also an idiot.

I had tried to show them I could do whatever they wanted, which for today was simply getting out of the chair. I wanted to show them I was in charge of myself, and with my renewed positive mood, I really thought it would go well. I was supposed to lift myself and stand under my own power. I was only supposed to stand, nothing more. They were explicit.

So here I go.

I manage, with amazing effort, to get myself onto my feet. The pain in my legs was legendary, but there I was, standing. As I'm doing this, the therapist is close by my side, clearly impressed, and she is giving me all sorts of encouragement. She was great. Don't forget, I've only been in the gym a few times before, and I had only just arrived for this session. I'm looking like Superman here, a shaking and sweaty hero, who is very much upright and very much standing.

Then I decide to show them my big Superman brain.

Against all rational logic, against the desire of my shrunken and humiliated legs who want nothing more than to sit down, I decide to take a step. A big one. Thrilled by my first victory over gravity, I didn't give such a huge challenge a second thought.

Brilliantly, I lean forward and command my legs to move, expecting I would be able to walk.

My upper body leans way out in front of my hips and I feel gravity taking a renewed interest in me. Already I'm feeling vertigo. Looking at my therapist, I see my therapist's shocked awareness as she realizes what I'm trying to do. Immediately I feel her body against mine, warm and solid, as she tries to support my weight. The look on her face is a strange mix of panic and pain, which makes me think she knew what was coming. Meanwhile, as the vertigo and my therapist take firmer hold of me, I try in vain to make my leg swing out in front of me, to take that step. No love. My leg is a tree trunk. My leg is in another room having a nap. My leg ignores me utterly.

That was when gravity decided if my legs won't help me, it would. I start to fall.

My therapist, committed to saving me from the floor, holds on tightly to my gown, but the effect is hardly helpful. In spite of her support, my flimsy green non-clothing, and my modesty, are torn from me in an instant. Luckily, my gown being ripped from my body has the effect of spinning me around, so the man with one decent arm, no legs to speak of, and a very bad case of dizziness, is entirely naked and spinning as he falls.

I am the grotesque ballerina, and this dance is dedicated to landing. I want to make this show one to remember.

I hit the ground turned nearly all the way around, landing on my shoulder and side.

I don't remember any pain, mostly because of the loud noise filling my head. The final step of my dance was my skull meeting the floor. I was out cold. I can only imagine the panic this scene must have caused amongst the staff.

When meat ARRIVES damaged, they are happy to fix it. That is what this particular place of worship does. However, when meat in their care is damaged AFTER it arrives, things like lawyers and lawsuits happen. They don't like having to fix those quite as much.

When I woke up, I found new tubes in me and pain in new places. I can see my legs are swollen again, and my bad arm is a screaming cluster of obscenities, each one more interesting and creative than the last.

Screw the plan, I want some fog. I need my pain meds.

Interestingly, in spite of my massive headache and the universe of new afflictions, I still feel pretty good. I still feel like me. A me that is fighting back tears from grotesque pain and humiliation, but still me. I think this is a good sign.

A nurse walks into my room with a look of apology in her eyes, and I can see she is here to deliver a dose of pain killer. What wonderful timing. Sheet goes up, sheet goes down, and I'm already feeling better. Except for her, I haven't seen anyone in my room for a while. After they were certain I had done no permanent damage to myself, they pretty much left me to recover on my own. Now that I've had a shot I can feel the morphine tide rising, and I examine my thoughts as they try to surface.

I look out my window and let myself wander.

I think pain can be considered a religion, so long as we realize religion is something we choose to submit to. To be subdued by pain is similar to being controlled by a church. You give up your ability to think rationally, and allow others to plant dogma and ideology into your daily consciousness in its stead. I give up my logical self while the pain has me in its grip, and I think of nothing else but to do as the pain demands. To be its servant. To submit and to serve.

Isn't that the goal of all religion?

I think about men and women, and of the pain we've endured as a species for the benefit of religion. We have not been well-served. Yet in spite of the evidence of so much anguish, so much needless suffering, I wonder why more of us never seemed to notice.

What does a church want from a man? A woman? What did the old gods want? What about the cash god and its steely-eyed church of the economy? What does this new god want?

I've always thought when it comes to the men, both the old and new gods want nothing more than to keep them busy. Scores of them, working hard doing jobs that will benefit the church, to increase the bottom line. Men who are busy have no time to get into trouble, and by that I mean they won't have time to wonder why they're working so hard while achieving so little.

The old and the new gods alike want nothing less than total control - absolute submission. That's why, if you look back, one sees the classic male breadwinner who is forced to work himself into an early grave. The crazy part, as I see it, is that when asked to do so, he will also offer himself up as canon fodder, where for even less reward he is allowed to die alone, far from his wife and children - far from his life, for a cause that probably doesn't concern him, or anyone he knows.

The pope wanted land and wealth, so the serfs were ordered to take up arms. Today, when the economy needs resources, men are conscripted and sent overseas to die, to enforce a more compliant brand of peace upon resource rich lands.

Men kept busy, at work or at war.

How can this possibly be good for humanity?

It's even worse for the women.

With only one exception, pretty much every religion I've ever heard of sees women as very little more than 'ambulatory uteri.' If they can be trained to work, even better. The only exception is the church of cash.

The God of Cash sees women as human resources, to be harvested and used in exactly the same way as the males, but it sees their uteri as an enemy of productivity, and therefore something that should be shunned. To money, the ideal women is hard working and sterile. Future generations are not its problem.

I can see this in a hundred different ways in our culture. Count the ways childless couples are better off. Men, free from the burden of a womb, are able to keep the money gods happy simply by showing up for work every day, meanwhile their wives have to ensure they don't participate in something as inconvenient as childbirth, and if they do, they'd better be sure it doesn't interfere with productivity in the workplace.

What is the history of consumer culture in North America, if not the story of turning one gender into a parody of the other so that both work hard and spend the money they earn on junk?

More importantly, how is making women ashamed to have children supposed to be good for our culture? For our species?

Men and women both suffer consequences for the rebellious act of procreation, but while the impact on the man's work life is negligible, the woman is effectively removed from the workforce during the process. So knowing that, why is it society makes so many women feel like they have to choose between a dignified productive life, or a child?

Of course, it will be argued western churches encourage family values, but what are those values?

Women as chattel? Women who may be shunned if they choose to have children alone or for another family? The great religions have a long history of wanting to keep women subdued and submissive, just like the men. The ironic thing is, in both cases they have used 'labour' to do it.

Manual labour for the men and birthing labour for the women.

The morphine tide rises and falls quickly some days, and after this morning the tide has gone out very quickly indeed. I try to keep my thoughts steady, but the pain in my legs is distracting me.

As I think about the genders, I know I'm biased. Not just because I'm male, but also because of my age. My generation, the kids who grew up in the seventies, had to endure all sorts of turmoil when it came to gender. The so-called gender wars, which I think represented the end-times of a woman's ability to chose femininity, were fought in my childhood. Bugs Bunny and Jane Fonda shared air time Saturday mornings. As I grew up, I watched as women lobbied to become the equals of men in the work force, only to see them become just as constrained, just as limited by their success. Yet somehow, in the face of this new and onerous expectation, they still had to face the difficulties of being a woman.

The God of Cash didn't want to liberate women, so much as add another layer of servitude to the duties the old gods had already imposed.

For the men, there isn't really any parallel. We are expected to help out more, but what man can breast feed?

My legs ache and I'm restless. Life doesn't need to be this way. I don't think men and women have to service anyone else's ideas regarding gender if they choose not to.

The God of Cash gives power to those who serve him. He rewards theft and dishonesty more than rational thought or constructive labour, so the society the money god creates, has created, is always going to have an overt anti-human veil. Fundamentally, at its core, it will be evil.

Evil being defined as whatever is bad for the species and its progress.

Some women feel obligated to shun motherhood. Some men to shun fatherhood. The family is ostracized as an inconvenient fact of life that must be tolerated. Discouraged whenever possible. The economic classes rarely work together for common gain, but instead fight one another. The powerful harvest the resources of the less powerful at their leisure, without thought to consequences, and those who are being harvested scrap among themselves for whatever remains.

How is that good for the species?

I look out my window, sore and tired, and realize I'm railing against my entire society. I'm pretty much saying both the church and the state are broken and they need to change, and since they aren't doing it voluntarily they need to be pushed.

By who?

I think the only people capable of stepping up and changing this broken world are the atheists. The humanists. All those among the population, living under whatever tag they've chosen, who have liberated themselves from the belief gods are somehow in charge. Be they gods of legend, or myth, or of some antiquated book selectively interpreted by ambitious men, or the crass modern God of Cash. My vision of the future is where men and women see each other as people first and reproductive organs second. This world will be made to grow and thrive through people who define each other by their abilities, both demonstrated and potential, and not the ones attributed to them based on gender.

They won't see a job that must be done by a man or a woman, they will see a job.

I hope they see this one.

As I heal, I've grown more and more afraid of religion.

All of them. Every single one.

I think of our history and of what we've done to ourselves, and I can't help but think religion is the greatest evil ever visited upon us.

Minds created nuclear weapons, but religions tell us we have the divine right to use them. What is religion but a way to separate those who deserve to live from those who don't?

My sculpture sits unmoved as I watch it through my window, the clouds changing the shadows as they pass overhead. My arm is still really sore, my legs an endless source of distraction, and my thoughts are everywhere. I'll have to accept it. I'm finding the pain from the fall too much to ignore.

I can tell the day is going to pass slowly in the ward. Just me and my thoughts, watching the universe through my window.

The idea an atheist would never do anything selfish or irrational is pretty absurd, but I like to believe if they did, they would at least understand why.

"There would be that missing element of truth. No gods means no-one to blame."

I speak the words into my room, but Hellen refuses to answer. I know she is dead, and I know what I'm seeing is not her, but in spite of my fear I want to help her.

Her apparition has come fully unhinged, and it's clear she is loosing her mind.

I close my eyes and see myself rising from the bed. I'm strong again, powerful and in charge. Hellen stands in the corner, her clothes shredded and her eyes red. Her anger radiates into the room like heat off an engine. I walk towards her, my steps confident, and when I arrive, I reach out with my two good hands and take hers. They send a chill through me. I grip them tightly and look at her face, at her body. She glares at me, the hatred so powerful it washes over my skin like waves on the ocean. A tide that strips our humanity to the bone.

I lean over and tenderly kiss her forehead. My lips rest on her cold skin, and patiently I wait ... I hope ... for her to change.

In bed with my eyes closed I face her, waiting, and then I feel it - warmth. I open my eyes and look at her, still standing alone in the corner. She's changed. Her clothing has been mended and her eyes are no longer sunken and red. The scarf I bought her for Christmas is fresh and new, and she looks young again.

*"I don't understand."*

"Don't worry. I think it means you've been saved."

# 26
AUGUST 25, NOON

My bird has returned.

The sun is high above us, and he has been perched here for hours, on the same branch outside my window, just as he was all those weeks ago. This is the first time he's been back since the cat incident, and I was glad to see him. After a few days had passed I had no expectation he would ever return. I spotted him almost the moment I woke up, and I spent the half hour before breakfast watching him. Just as before, he jumped from one spot to the next, and in between each hop performed that weird beak-cleaning ritual.

As the orange light took hold of the day, my breakfast having come and gone, he started to sing. Sharp, room-filling notes. Up and down. Long trills and short whistles. It seemed like he was having a great time, and I found myself caught up in his tune.

He occasionally repeated one particular refrain that consisted of two short staccato notes plus a longer one just a bit higher up the scale. I tried to whistle it but it was an exercise in futility. My lips are still quite unreliable, so I quickly gave that idea a pass. I started to sing the notes instead.

I haven't been doing a lot of talking since my jaw was released and because of that my voice was not very strong. I put in a lot of crackling effort but I got very little joy from the sounds. I couldn't match his notes, not at all, and in a short time my tune started to wander a bit.

Then something happened. Something opened inside of me, and I found myself inside the notes, inside the tune, and I began to feel the music come of itself. Without help from my bird or any sort of musical logic, notes began to come to me. Melodies, entire rhythms, all of them letting themselves out through me.

I was released, and before long the emotions took over.

Initially I was barely whispering. I doubt anyone else would have been able to hear me unless they were right there next to me, but I gained confidence, and the emotion I was holding inside started to demand access to the notes.

I wasn't about to deny them the chance.

From my strained whispers came lightness, the tentative sounds I was making becoming powerful, and soon I was singing wordless songs to my room, the walls under assault from the organic logic of music.

My healed lungs filled with air and I let it all out of me - great winding songs that spoke of love and loss. It was only notes, just notes, but they told stories of heroes and rescue. The dam within me, that comfortable barrier against myself, had broken.

I wasn't singing anymore; I was performing. I've never been a singer, not once in my life, and yet today I was the centre of the world. My mouth was stretched wide. I was the sound and the fury and I let loose the dogs of war. I don't know what kind of singing it was but I was consumed by it, and the universe was rapt - the only witness to this grand acoustic birth.

A nurse walked in, the one with the french braid, and she stopped in her tracks at the sight of me. Part of me was aware of her but not enough to care, and I sang to her - a song of love and duty. She was transfixed as I sang for her a story in stanzas of brightness and colour, and I imagine she swooned while the sounds filled my head.

Soon, others came into the chamber, the auditorium, the grand hall, and my song surrounded them. Went through them. They held each other fast to the spot, so as to keep the song from sweeping them away.

My doctor, some interns, a patient from another room. The ward was drawn to me as I was taken by this release, held as I let all of the emotions go.

There was no logic to the music. No goal. It wandered and searched, exploring the darkest and most forgotten threads of our ancestral memory. It told of discoveries made and fortunes displayed. The greatness of infinity was splayed on the bed with me, and the thorns of the rose didn't stand a chance against the wine. A consummation happened, and we were the mortals who bore witness. Everyone heard it, it was too much to miss, and it kept coming. More song, more music, more truth.

I could feel a wetness on my cheeks as I shared this birth. Soon the tears flowed freely as I heralded the rise of we, the humans - the angels of the savannas. I foretold of disasters and gained access to the lost secrets of our progenitors. Our histories grew and I sang of the gods we created, of their temples and their shrines. The eons passed, and in time the guardians left the crypts. I sang as I pillaged their stolen icons, the temples of the gods falling to my vocal assault. I knew then they were gone forever. I stood over their memories and I sang their death song, the hard notes and graven images made into life and love. They could never have created such beauty without me.

Those gods passed into history, forgotten, and others came. I sang the song of hard-earned knowledge. Of wisdom. Truth and eventualities. I sang of the atoms that were split in the cause of war, and I sang of the victims.

I could feel my heart beating in my chest as I sang to the people I've loved and who are now gone, and I sang to those I will love in the future. My eyes ran with the waters inside of me and still I sang, the burnt wood smell of smoke and emotions filling the room.

My anger left me, and as it did I witnessed the walls of the churches tremble and fall, no match for this honesty. I bid my sorrows leave, and as the strength of my joy became clearer I watched the priests and the prophets, their gods and their immortals, bow their heads in regret at the failures they have sown among us. I broadcast my love, and from it the universe grew, expanded. Glowing colours and infinite heat returned for my efforts.

I gave my audience everything. My hatreds, my angers, my sorrows, my lusting thoughts of conquest and my cowardly tremblings in fear of my fate. I gave it all and the universe accepted everything without a word. Without a sound. Without judgement.

Then Hellen came. She stood in her corner, listening as I sang to her memory.

My Hellen, yours was the saddest refrain. I sang to our selfish wants and I sang to the fact we never allowed the other to exist. I sang to our pain and I sang to our deaths. I cried through the notes as the song aged, its passage through me coming to an end. The tide had risen, and it was time for the tide to fall - the day was finished, and I should let the sun go down.

Our love had its time but that time is done. I could see your tears, your tragic comprehension, and then I watched you leave.

The song, my song, began to grow quiet.

I could feel the emotions were nearly through with me, and an exhaustion started to take hold. My limbs were getting heavy, and I found my eyes wanted nothing more than to rest, to close themselves against the world and its realities. Let the sun go down. Let it fade for tomorrow.

I could hear my breath, my consciousness of air. A single note remained, and it wanted to hold on as long as it could.

So soft, so very quiet, and I don't know if I was making a sound at all. I could feel it though, the note deep inside, gripping me, and I wanted it to stay. It was beautiful, and I needed that beauty with me. To become me. I opened up my throat and let it come out, into this little world, this minuscule universe I created.

I closed my eyes. The song was finished and the silence that filled my mind became as beautiful as the song, and it spoke to me in words that implied eternities. This understanding had never planned on staying with me, but for the time it was here, during the time I was the song, I was the measure of beauty in this universe.

For that, I don't think I can ever be afraid again.

I rested in bed for a short while, feeling warm and safe and clean. I could hear the people in my room as they made their way back to the day, back to their coffee and their routines. When I finally opened my eyes my audience was gone and I could see my bird sitting on the branch. A little yellow bird. My friend, swaying gently on his perch in the sun, and in my mind I thanked him. I thanked him with my entire being for doing this for me. I thanked him for giving me my new voice.

"Thank you Soleil."

My little yellow friend deserves a name.

# 27

## AUGUST 25, EVENING

Dinner is served, and I'm rewarded for my ongoing progress with broccoli, potatoes, a thin slab of gravy moistened beef, and the usual green gelatin. I really don't like the milk here because it always seems old. They assure me it's not, but I get the apple juice instead.

After my great awakening this morning, the day continued in a fairly normal way. Physio therapy came and went, and I lived through it with only minor emotional scarring. The counsellor seemed willing to believe I was not completely insane, and I had a chance to speak with my doctor. In spite of my not being able to stand without a lot of help, he has agreed to reduce the amount of morphine I'm getting. After the fall the other day it looked as if I might never get off the stuff, but this morning has made me feel more optimistic. I'm looking forward to the day when I'll be able to reminisce about the time in my life I took so many pain meds.

As I eat, I can see the effect my performance has had. The ward is more lively than usual, more animated. I can sense it in a dozen different little ways, and together they make a big difference. I see smiles instead of blank institutional masks. People are addressing one another more easily, and the patients who visited seem less upset. I know I did that, and I'm glad. The friendlier mood suits this place, this normally sterile and inhuman place, and I hope it lasts. I've also noticed the greatest change seems to have been reserved for me.

I am no longer meat.

In our great public medical institutions, the status of meat is bestowed on all of the patients the moment they arrive. Not even the staff is entirely immune, and yet today I've apparently risen above it. When I speak, it's with the authoritative voice of a person, and people answer me with deliberation and care. I can hear it in the briefest of pauses before they respond. The fact they are listening to me at all makes me feel good, because it's not normal for the grievances of meat to get a lot of attention.

As I think about how I feel, this emotional warmth of being understood and appreciated, its novelty makes me aware we are institutionalized everywhere, in every aspect of our daily life. Our entire existence is spent managed by others, pacified by others, but to whose benefit? I speak of the grievances of meat, but have my grievances been well-received by the society I live in?

Digesting this thought, I'm find myself acutely aware of the obvious parallels between my status here in this hospital as numbered meat, and my previous status as a numbered citizen.

I realize I was no better off before the accident, at least not when I consider my place in society. I was just another warm body earning food and shelter by being useful, in my case by driving other warm bodies around all day, and that was that. Marriage allowed me to overlook the truth of a hopeless working reality, but what of those without the gift of luck. What of them? Lives spent working to achieve the impossible dream of freedom, a liberty so foreign most of us wouldn't know what to do with it, with the overall effect making each of us into just one more worthless citizen.

A worthless citizen. It seems so tragic and feels so true.

So many corporations using our labour, using our knowledge and our ingenuity, to create such wonderful junk - and we covet it. We crave the result of our efforts for the company. We become willing slaves to our debts as we return to them our pay, and more, to acquire the very things we worked so hard to create. We manufacture our shackles and then stand in line among friends, waiting for our turn to wear them. They have us producing shiny trinkets, which we enslave ourselves to own.

We, as individuals, don't really exist when thought of in those terms. We are the microscopic specks of pigment that create the epic painting, each one becoming meaningless when removed from the context of the whole. The loss of an individual would never be noticed, the canvas would be identical in every way.

How is it I'm only figuring this out now? How could I have lived my entire life thinking I mattered to the world, when in reality my importance was illusory, limited only to those in direct contact with me?

Oddly enough, it now seems pretty obvious to me. I can see I didn't lose any sort of status when I arrived here. I actually gained it. I went from being one among millions to one in just a few dozen, and instead of having huge nameless organizations working to keep me content and docile, I have individuals doing it. People with names I can learn.

I can see when I leave here I'll be unrecognizable to anyone who knew me before.

Like so many of the things I've come to understand since my arrival, I'm glad to have gained this new perspective, but I'm more curious about how it could have happened. How could millions of individuals, men and women who are used to asking and getting, become so unimportant, so disposable, to our society? Perhaps more importantly, how could they, how could we, put people in power who clearly view us as cattle? Our leaders are supposed to be people whose sole purpose is the furtherance of the common good, and yet their actions show such a clear disdain for us, for our needs, it simply cannot be hidden. Realistically, it's not like they are even trying. The word politician is synonymous with liar.

How is it possible we accept that?

But the answer is obvious, isn't it?

A lie that gives false hope is better than a reality which provides none, so we are happy to believe their lies, as long as we think we will get what we want. Hope. Another obvious truth hidden in plain sight.

The convoluted obfuscation that is 'Fair Trade' coffee comes immediately to my mind.

Anyone who has ever purchased coffee labelled 'Fair Trade' probably imagined they were doing the world a bit of good, and yet, I would argue they were accepting a lie, more likely many lies, to get something they wanted.

When they paid for that coffee, the coffee that was supposed to have been harvested by labour guaranteed to be getting a wage sufficient to support themselves and their families, did they ever look across the muffin display at the person who handed it to them? That person right there, right there in their face, the person whose odour would be available to them if they just leaned a little bit further over the counter. Is that person making enough money to raise a family? Are they earning enough money to even consider a family?

Of course they aren't. They're getting minimum wage.

Minimum being the operative word.

So we get our coffee with a clean conscience, as long as we are willing to overlook the person who hands it to us.

What about organic foods, hybrid cars, low power lighting? The lies that allow us to feel good exist there as well. The lies are not even well-hidden.

It seems bizarre, so few people notice these things, and yet I've done it a thousand times myself. I'm probably doing it right now, in a hundred ways I haven't even realized.

When it comes to people's unconscious desire to believe lies, I think maybe bus drivers have a unique perspective. How about the person who wants to know when the next bus is coming? Every driver knows this routine, and I think it's a great example of how we generally want to be lied to.

This happens all the time. A passenger, usually clutching a schedule, is waiting at a stop wanting to know about the bus after mine. My bus is full and this passenger doesn't want to ride crammed together with so many strangers. They are hoping the next bus will be less full, and what they want from me is a guarantee the next bus will arrive when scheduled. Bus drivers know where this is going. As a driver, I simply cannot guarantee anything. Granted, most drivers simply tell them the next bus is on time and leave it at that, but I'm not most drivers. I don't like to assume it will arrive on time, only to have the next driver arrive ten minutes late and get abused needlessly. So I tell them the truth, I do not know, and judging from the traffic it seems unlikely. This generally infuriates most people, and after a few seconds of being told I'm unfit to serve the public I close the door and leave.

These passengers aren't stupid. They ask me if the next bus will be on time in spite of having already read the schedule, and in spite of being able to see the same crush of rush hour traffic as I can. They can also see how full my bus is, and the fact the next bus will likely be just as jam-packed. It seems pretty obvious.

They know everything I know, they can see everything I can see, and yet they ask me to tell them a story. A happy story where they won't be late, and their favourite seat is always empty. These passengers want that guarantee from me because they need that lie. They need me to say everything will be alright.

And what happens when it isn't?

I have to wonder. Does a person believe the lies, when they know them for what they are? I suspect the answer has something to do with how much you want something to be true.

If a politician (while campaigning to get elected) says he can fix your city and make it crime free, he has, at that moment, only one concern. He must, above all, be the most sincere and believable messenger he can be. That's it. That's all. He isn't thinking about creative and effective plans to make your city crime free, or what is causing the crime, or even if there is anything he can realistically do.

No.

His only goal is to make you believe his lie.

Once we allow ourselves to believe, then even if we fully understand how most crime has its roots in soil much deeper than a single term of office, the debate ends. He got our vote. The bait has been taken, and we are caught. Hook, line and sinker.

That phrase means something. We allow ourselves to be lied to, to be harvested because we believe it gets us something we want. It's that simple.

In the case of the politician, we are contributing to the abolition of crime in our cities. As time makes the impossibility of this goal clearer, we can console ourselves by saying it must be the politician's fault, not ours. He is clearly too corrupt himself, or too soft, or too misguided. We would be wrong to think those things, but we do.

By the millions.

In this bed, I'm not really able to lie to myself about much. The last time I did, I found myself on the floor unconscious. But, in the real world, do our lies have the same sort of immediate consequences?

I suspect yes, but due to the vastness of our society we are able to disconnect ourselves from it and blame a personified 'society' in our heads.

I am society. You are society. Which one of us is at fault?

We both are.

In our current society, our ills are often of our own making, but we don't want to admit it, so we blame our leaders. Their job is to take that blame, and then fade into obscurity when their term in office is done. Fade away with the millions of dollars we begrudgingly gave them. Is it any surprise the vast majority of us are invisible? Disposable? Is it really such a great stretch to understand why a politician can view us as myopic and self-serving, and by their actions condemn us for it?

As I ponder this, I realize politicians treating the 'little people' as dirt is not a vice; it's a defence mechanism. One established early in their careers as they realize the world is not going to respect or reward them for their noble goals. Only cash will give them the power to make the smallest of changes, but cash has an agenda. It always does.

That doesn't leave us much, does it? Our society is not structured to work for its citizens, and even our leaders are held hostage by the money that puts them in power. By my definition, this means our society is broken.

The needs of the species are not properly served by our current institutions, so they must be changed.

The morality of beauty is offended by what we have created, and as we plead ignorance, the bombs we build continue to fall. Killing our enemies will make it better. It will make everything right again.

As Hellen liked to say, they are homeless because they are lazy.

If we are going to survive as a species, we need to evolve. We need to see the real world - the one without gods, or humanity will fall.

# SEPTEMBER 21 — 28

Today I've been told I'll take a step, and I'm starting to believe it's possible.

Markus came by earlier today and we chatted about my future here. He seems to think I'll be discharged in about three weeks, four at the outside, at which point the hospital will set me up with a homecare provider. My understanding is an assistant will come for a period of time each day to help me prepare meals and do laundry. Things like that. The help will last for a few weeks, maybe a month or two.

After that I'll be pretty much on my own.

My arm has been feeling good the last few days so I'm not too worried about cooking for myself. I use the hand exerciser for a few hours each day, and the effect from this extra effort makes me optimistic. My legs are another matter.

Today I'm supposed to walk, and although I feel much better, a part of me is worried. That fall last week was impressive and I don't want to repeat it. Physio says it won't happen, so I'm going to have to trust my therapist. I saw the rig they use, parallel bars as far as I can tell. It looks like I'll be walking along using my arms to support me.

That should be fun. If my bad arm fails I get to collapse in a heap.

Markus won't be back for at least an hour, and I once again turn inward. I've passed a great deal of time exploring my obsession, but I can't help wondering if what I'm attributing to atheism isn't simply something that could be more accurately thought of as an attribute of all introspective and thoughtful humans. I think so. It allows us our humanity while keeping the lack of any sort of belief out of the equation. I can be a human with no beliefs in any gods, and that means I can be whatever I choose. I can be the great benefactor of mankind serving the needs of humanity, or I could be an evil and unthinking bastard. My choice.

As I try to visualize our successful ascension to grace, I imagine this futuristic Utopia as a society not too different from our own. The biggest difference will have to do with priorities. What I see is a culture that has entirely different priorities.

If a society were to value something other than its cash gods, what would it look like? If the god was made to serve the citizens, or better yet eliminated entirely, would the people of the world be allowed to rise to greater heights, or would the God of Cash just find new ways to enslave them?

Probably a bit of both.

Morality is a big part of the solution because it directs priorities, and for that reason I think morality should be based on beauty. With beauty as the metric, things become intuitive and instinctual.

A man beating a child is an evil and ugly act, but a man teaching a child is beautiful. The good of our actions and the greatness of our spirit are the things we search for in poetry and art. When we find them we feel as though we have transcended our physical selves, becoming something more. It is within that 'more' the morality of humanity rests.

Clearly I'm oversimplifying things, but wouldn't that make more sense than the crippled industrialized moralities at war with one another today? What humanity thinks of as morality, over most of the globe, is based entirely on Bronze-Age mythologies. Even our concept of commerce came from that backwater of history.

Beauty and art have value, and we as a species need to find a way to make that value more apparent.

I visualize an office. The walls are filled with awards, the air thick with cigar smoke and cynicism. At an old desk sits 'The Editor.' He is the keeper of clarity and reason, and his red pen is not a tool for making friends. Wizened from the hardships of scotch and aggressive wordplay, he reviews my thoughts. In the margin he writes 'good luck pal.'

I can't help but grin. I know he's right.

The joys of healing. I spend most of my time playing with society; worlds built and destroyed while I wait for Markus. He's late, and I'm anxious to get there today because as much as I'm not looking forward to the struggle, I really want to see what I can do.

I've become an expert at passing time. I glance out the window to see if I'll get another visit from Soleil. I don't see him, so my eyes wander further out to my park.

As I expected, the fall colours look spectacular. The maples near my sculpture are quickly turning a deep ochre. It's stunning to see through the branches, as the sun starts its gentle arc towards the earth. They seem to glow, the light reflecting lustrously from the leaves, luminous and ethereal.

My sculpture is alone. They fixed the light a few days ago and the nighttime halo has been restored fully. In fact, I can see the colours of the trees surrounding it are enhancing the effect, making the warmth of the bronze bleed into the surrounding life. The scene makes me remember my views on nature, and the bronze made by we, the clever apes, holds my imagination fast.

We are a beautiful species when we try.

I'm restored to my senses by Markus, who rushes into the room with a grin and a chair.

We work together quickly. I'm mostly lifted into the chair, and with practised efficiency he adjusts the saline tubes for safety and the blankets for modesty. Then we're off, rushing through the halls.

A few doors along, Markus stops and asks about my box of macaroni. I tell him I forgot it, and so we spin around and head back to the room, the race is clearly on. Nurses and patients tut-tut our reckless pace, and in no time we are back in my room, the box found and stowed. A quick turn and we are back on our way.

The green walls roll past us and the doors mark our progress like telephone poles on the highway. My head hangs backwards, and memories of looking out the rear window of my father's Trans Am comfort me. I count the pillars as they pass.

Arriving in the gym, the clock tells me we are not that late. Ten minutes, which by hospital standards means we are right on time. On the other side of the room is my therapist, Lacy. She doesn't wear makeup, relying instead on her physique to make an impression. Unlike so many of the therapists, Lacy uses all the exercise equipment her patients use. She is in incredible shape, and it shows. I've caught Markus giving her the eye more than once, and it occurs to me he should be more respectful. It's one thing to admire a person for their physical appearance, but it's quite another to ogle them like a buffet.

Lacy takes control of the chair from Markus and I watch from inches away as they exchange a very personal look. Did I really just see that? I would never have guessed, but apparently they are a couple. That explains his somewhat lewd behaviour. I do the mandatory ring check, and of course they have matching wedding bands. Unless I'm advised otherwise, I'm going to have to conclude they are married. I think that's an amazing thing, to be able to work together like this, and it explains the involvement Markus has had in my recovery.

"Got the box?" Lacy asks me.

"Right here. What's up?" I reply.

She pushes my chair under the parallel bars, and that's when I notice the equipment above it. A giant electric winch of some sort, complete with a body harness and steel cables. It looks like the type of rig I imagine they use to make kung-fu movies. I think of the last time I watched a martial artist run weightless over top a bamboo forest and the nonsensical phrase 'all hail to the gibberish kick' pops into my head. She starts to hook me in, and as usual, I find myself once again in the position of abandoning all modesty to get into some sort of medical situation.

Injured is bad enough. Naked and injured is much worse.

Thankfully, after I'm secured, Lacy returns my mock clothing to me, draping it over my body and the harness.

"Let's see the box," she says.

I hold it up for her, and without the slightest hesitation she takes it from my hand and tosses it carefully to the other end of the parallel bars.

"I don't expect you to pick it up, but if you can't walk over and kick it with your toe today, it stays there until you can."

She said it with a grin, and I can see Markus off to the side, pretending to work on some cables. He is giggling quietly to himself.

The expression 'physical terrorists' was one I had heard before, and always from people who've had to deal with the profession Lacy calls home. Now I know why. The bars are easily ten feet long, probably twenty, and I have not yet managed to take a single step. The thought of what is to come already has me sweating. I can see this is going to be tough.

As I half-stand, half-dangle, Lacy stands a few feet in front of me, hands on her hips, waiting for me to start.

I can feel the pain already, in my legs, in my side, and unexpectedly I notice a small tattoo on her hip. A telescope. It's plain but attractive, and I welcome the distraction. I focus on its shape as I straighten my legs, the weight of my body forcing my calves and thighs to adjust. My palms sweat morphine into the wood as I adjust my grip. Willing myself forward, through the muscular fog of lost nerve endings, I start to move my right leg. My knees twitch unsteadily. My foot slides an inch or two over the industrial flooring and I start to sweat in earnest. My arms are already shaking from the effort, and I know I'm going to have a bad day. I look at the tattoo on Lacy's hip, partly hidden by her index finger, and I force my legs to move, to work, as I try to send it my pain. My arms and legs grow hot as I commune with the ink on her skin, in the room whose lights are getting too bright, and I'm going to make this work.

That box is my teddy bear, and I want it back.

# SEPTEMBER 2   29

I woke up this morning to the sound of my voice, speaking my dream into the room. I distinctly heard the phrase "We've traded the monks who were pious for the monks who yell pay us!"

Once I was awake enough to realize what I had done, I wished I could remember more. It must have been a good one.

I'm feeling stronger. Next to me is my somewhat abused box of macaroni. It took me almost the entire ninety minutes, but I was able to drag this sorry thing I call my body all the way down the track to kick it. Actually, I didn't kick it. I nudged it, really gently, with the toe that hurt the least. The effort cost me three pounds, what looked like three litres of sweat, plus a special dose of 'Gluteus Maximus' brand pain killer. I sweat so much they put a special carpet under me on the track, otherwise I would have been in danger of slipping. That winch? The harness? They did nothing, not really. While I walked, struggled, swore, cried, bled and aged, the rigging was set to allow me to fall almost to my knees before it would support my weight. I would have been lucky to escape with just a set of really sore ribs if I had actually fallen.

I make it sound bad, but I'm actually quite proud. I look out the window to send the news to my sculpture, and my bronze totem is happy to hear it. Too bad Soleil isn't here. He would be glad for me too.

I wonder if Hellen would have been proud of me? I really don't know. I suppose she would have been, at some level, but a big part of me wonders if she would have stayed with me while I worked. I looked horrible. Lacy said later my colour was quite hectic, and I thought I was going to vomit on at least three occasions. These are not the conditions a woman like Hellen would tend to accept. I imagine she would have given me a small kick on the cheek and left me to fend for myself in the gym.

Did I really just say that?

Kiss. I meant to say kiss.

The leaves are becoming more impressive each day, and I'm getting my fill before they fall. My house, the one I bought after Hellen and I split up, is in the city. It's a big brownstone, probably a hundred years old with no back yard, but it's near downtown. Unfortunately, the most life you'll ever find near its ancient concrete foundation is either the struggling efforts of sidewalk moss, or the occasional random stray leaf. They fall from the decorative trees planted by the city alongside the road. The trees never last long, which isn't really a surprise when you realize they're forced to live through Friday night drunks who tear at their branches, herds of early morning dogs who dig at their roots, and the choking exhaust from morning and evening rush hours. I drove the bus route which passes my house for many years before I moved there, and in that time I've seen them replace those trees at least twice. In hindsight I have to wonder why I went there to find a place at all. I'm not a fan of smog-induced sterility.

It occurs to me Hellen and her family never traded monks. They worshipped both. Pay us and pious alike. I'll probably have that line in my head all day. I don't have physio, and I remember Markus has the day off, so I'm alone once again with my thoughts.

I've noticed my doctor acting differently. He sees me as a completed work, and all he's waiting for is a buzzer to go off to tell him to take me out of the oven. The somewhat impatient answers to my questions, or the fast rounds where he simply peeks his head in the door, it's telling me I've been here a long time and he's anxious to send me home.

I hear heart surgery patients are expected to walk the day of their surgery and leave the hospital usually within just a few more. When Hellen had her breast implants replaced with the safer saltwater variety, she was made to walk within an hour of waking up. That was hell to watch, but it was nothing next to her recovery. I'll just say I have a far better understanding of the mindset of plastic surgeons, and especially their rush to get women outfitted with those things, considering what patient and doctor are expected to do for physical therapy.

I wish I could remember that dream. It seemed so vivid, and of course now that I'm awake it's simply melted into the oblivion of my soupy morning thoughts. I still like the line, at least that didn't leave me, but without context it's just a cute little joke. A cipher that tells me nothing but the punch line.

It was something about banks. Money.

I was starving when I woke up and breakfast was not nearly enough for me. I have my appetite back, and that's good, because I saw myself in one of the mirrors yesterday. The hospital gym is typical in that the walls are lined with those big dance studio mirrors. When I had finally arrived at the far end of the parallel bars, sweating and feeling very nearly dead, I made the mistake of looking up.

I nearly choked.

I'm a wraith. A skeleton. My legs look straighter, but my whole frame is wasted. Unused. I feel so strong, and my arm is responding so well to all my work, and yet when I saw myself I couldn't see anything on me that could be mistaken for muscle.

Nothing.

That's how I know I lost three pounds. I asked Markus how much I weighed and he couldn't remember, so after we were done he wheeled me onto a scale. Some quick math put me at 132 pounds. When he said the number I had to hold back tears.

Before the accident I worked out regularly. I was an avid cyclist and swimmer. I wasn't lean the way an athlete in training might be, but I was well muscled and I did keep my body fat levels within healthy limits.

I usually weighed somewhere near 200 pounds, give or take.

My life is so changed, so altered, and after all this time it just keeps reminding me, in such painful and creative ways. Novel and frustrating ways. I suppose I should be glad I didn't go right off the deep end, or at least if I have, I've been lucky enough to remain ignorant while afflicted.

"Governments are run by banks, so governments can never be made accountable to the people. It's the banks that must therefore be made accountable, in order that governments will follow." I listen to my voice echo off the sterile walls. Someone in my dream said that to me.

A shadow on brick. The dream reveals a shape.

I still don't remember anything specific, but that part fits my recollection. It had something to do with someone I was supposed to find, and I was approaching all the wrong people.

The monk bit is obvious at least. We traded the church for Wall Street, and the bankers have betrayed us utterly ... but perhaps betrayed is the wrong word. We expected them to behave similarly to our old gods, our old religions, and they didn't. How could they? They serve a god who, like time, simply doesn't exist.

Money doesn't exist. That was part of it. Of course the old gods didn't exist either, but they were never able to manifest themselves in our world with the force and savagery money can. Back in the days of religion, money was actually a token, a representation, a promise that the equivalent of something of value was somewhere accessible, and if the note was presented to the right leader, the right king, then that commodity, that something, could be obtained. Not a great explanation, but we (in the west) eventually called it the gold standard and it kept the money god tame and in line.

Other cultures used other commodities, like salt, but they all served the same purpose.

The connection to the real world made the cash god a limited god, and its wings were forever clipped. Its flights limited to what we mortals could invent or produce.

But then we left the gold standard and made banks the ultimate keepers of the cash. After that, virtual cash became like water, flowing freely from a ceaseless spigot. Numbers, so large our minds could hardly comprehend them, became the figures tossed across the globe every second. They represented the debts of a thousand governments, owed to the pan-national banks and the pan-national corporations, for services said to have been rendered.

Debt must be repaid, and from that truth the banks gained their power.

Meanwhile, our money, or more accurately its value, no longer exists in any form other than what a corporation or a bank decides. Our money is just another stock, another equity, rising and falling endlessly, representing the perceived value of our government's available resources, namely its citizens.

We, the worthless citizens, have simply become another equity, and like all stocks, if the supply is nearly infinite the value approaches zero.

The dream still hasn't come back to me, but I remember how it made me feel. I was furious and scared. It was the knowledge of our worth that infuriated me, frightened me, because in my dream the people in charge of our world: the politicians, the gangsters, the tycoons of business and religion, they all knew. They knew the truth in my dream, and they know the truth outside my window. They know right now as I heal, and they are doing nothing about it.

Nothing.

The powers-that-be worked to unleash this financial war on the citizens of the world, and to celebrate their silent victory, they harvest everything they can. We are the crop.

In my dream I could see it all, and awake I can see it even more clearly. A tightness appears in my chest as I come to understand humanity is being killed. We are being euthanized like cattle for nothing more noble than profit. Millions of families starve. Millions of humans live without shelter or medicines. A hundred million lifetimes of work are stolen in a fraction of a second, and the thieves, the corporations, the banks, the conglomerates, are all known to the police. Known, and never arrested.

Who is there to put in jail, if the killers are also the kings?

I woke up with a joke on my lips, and now I'm enraged. I don't understand why I had thought it was amusing.

The old churches might have been bad for our species, an evil perhaps unparalleled in our history, but they needed us. To make their ecumenical business model work we had to be allowed to breed, to make the worshippers who would pay into the collection plate. But the cash god, released upon us by the foolish greed of its worshippers, has no such need of us. We are simply a resource to be consumed, and the pain and suffering and death caused by the actions of its followers are all just inconsequential collateral damage - a side effect of the business model they worship.

It could be argued the old priests sometimes tried to do good, even while their actions oftentimes hurt us, but our new priests, these new monks who drive engineered sculptures to their churches and never allow our dirty light in, they rarely do any good at all. It's not profitable.

For our species to live, for humans to survive at any level, money and commerce and the business models they rely on must be made to serve us. Not we them.

Above all else, business ideology has to have the greater good at its core, otherwise it will destroy us.

A truce must be called.

I'm getting uncomfortably warm thinking about this. The effort to pull the ideas back from the lost dream has upset me quite a bit. I'm tense. Agitated. My body wants to pace the room, to vent its anger at the floor and the walls. I find, more and more, ideas take hold of me.

The thoughts just flow, unhinged, through me and out to the world. This thin, clammy world.

I can barely understand where these thoughts come from, and as I recount them, they float, dizzy and soft above my head. Taunting me. I try to reach for them, to take hold of them and understand them better. They exhaust me. I'll spend the rest of my life trying to pin these thoughts down. Command them to make more sense.

A part of me feels like I already understand, but these ideas come to me so fast, it seems like I'm reading them from a book. The fact they barely make sense, that they are merely the border of a dangerous territory I've never visited, just makes me feel they're that much more correct.

Solid twisted steel, embedded in concrete, keeping the tower straight. The invisible truth.

I try to calm myself down a bit by breathing. I close my eyes, and try to forget my pains. My chest feels better than ever and I can feel my ribs stretch as my lungs fill with air.

I look at us, at humanity, and as my heart slows I can see.

We were the primates who invented the club. Fire. Our battles were for food and shelter, sex, and a territory near water.

Primitive but clever, our weapons evolved as our societies advanced. In time we realized war was wasteful and gods were invented to control us. These gods did their job admirably, but eventually even that was not enough, and so more powerful gods were made. Vengeful gods. Gods who could destroy cities with a look, and do it for the very smallest of slights.

And these gods were good, and the control they held over our animal selves lasted for thousands of years. We had sheathed our weapons in nobility and honour, and would only use them for the good of our vengeful gods.

Then we created the last, greatest, god.

This new god doesn't care about good or evil. He is his own end. He feeds on the hearts of the old gods for profit, turning them to his will, making their followers his own. These usurped worshippers, thinking they are somehow still serving the old gods, pray and pay, and they are glad in their hearts as they lose their homes because they know their god is testing them ... and as their loved ones die from curable diseases they know they deserve it, because they did not work hard enough to make enough money ... and as their pensions are looted and they feel the handcuffs close around their wrists, they learn to go against the new god, to protest, is a crime he demands retribution for.

You are now a criminal. We send criminals to hell.

## SEPTEMBER 5 — 30

I went outside today.

Markus asked a favour of the day nurse, and without any fanfare I was loaded into a chair and carted out the front door.

The sun, that friend whose number I seem to have forgotten, took liberties with my skin while I sat, and the geriatric crust I hardly knew I was wearing was joyfully burnt away. Then there was that smell, the hospital smell I could never get out of my nostrils and my thoughts, it left me for a time as I enjoyed the cooling fall air. I found it again later, after I was returned to my room. I took a deep breath when I sat on my bed and immediately my head filled with my familiar medical scent. I'm already missing the air and the sun, and I'm anxious for my next reprieve from this chemical chamber of horrors, this enforced isolation of my nose.

I was able to see my tree. It stood close to the building, and the large branch the cat and Soleil had shared seemed dangerously close to the glass. No other room had such a feature, and I was very lucky the branch hadn't been trimmed before I arrived. Judging from how close to the glass it is, I suspect it will be down within the year. Where would I have been without my little friend, visiting me while my body and mind healed? The height is impressive as well, and for that I have to send the cat a silent nod of admiration.

To risk a fall from that height just for a bird shows a rare commitment to lunch.

I'm getting stronger. My legs are taking the work, taking the exercise, and they are learning. Soon they will once again understand the language of motion smashed from their memory, and I'll be free to roam the foolish paths and dangerous avenues my mind has found so fascinating of late.

Even my body is starting to look better. I'm still a ghoul, but I'm a ghoul who could think himself worthy of love. My face is nearly untouched by scars, and the large scars on my body are healing cleanly. I'll have to invent stories to tell at the beach.

Thinking back, I remember how upset I was the morning of my last dream. Unfortunately, other than those few disturbing thoughts, nothing specific ever came back to me. But the anger the dream brought out in me, that stayed hot and dry under my skin long after I woke. I was bothered for days afterwards. It's still here, actually. I'm still upset at what I think are crimes against humanity being committed by the leaders of our nations, by our corporations and our religions.

I suspect having been outside has made me feel poetic, even maudlin, but in spite of that I can see I'm very different today than I was before Hellen died. None of my ideologies fit anymore, and I'm finding the moral clothing everyone else leaves for me to be thin and unimpressive. I want so much more, and I somehow feel I have the right to demand it. The current state of affairs in the world is unacceptable to me, and I find my rants bring less and less comfort. Comprehension. Understanding. They are no longer enough. I feel like I should be doing something.

All of my thinking about families, the species, our duty to our descendants, is this new attitude, this new frustrated perspective, in response to that? I suppose if it is I should be happy. To have an understanding is one thing, but to fail to act on it, what else could that be but a crime committed against yourself?

I can barely walk twenty feet and yet I feel like I can change the world. Like I need to.

Maybe I'm crazy. The endless drugs, the blunt force trauma and the ghost of Hellen, all of them conspiring to scramble my brain into a Pollock canvas, the random impersonations of crazy, but I don't think so. I think I was crazy before. I was a spectator at a rape, a leering ape holding his cell phone and saying nothing. I prided myself in not participating in the war against humanity, bragging about my non-involvement to anyone who would listen, and I somehow thought that was enough. It never dawned on me my silence was what allowed it to happen in the first place.

I thought being an atheist, being a humanist, was a passive belief affecting only me. It's not. It can't be.

The leaders of this world killed my wife, they almost killed me, and I let them.

No more.

I look at my room, the dingy painted walls supporting a perfect accident of geometry, and I close my eyes. I'm back outside, remembering. The heat of the sun on my arms and my face was so calming. The warmth and love of molecular matter, hurled through space, directed at me. I could feel myself trying to absorb it, to steep myself in it. We were meant to be outside, to live with ourselves in this light, and I hope I never feel the need to hide myself from the universe again. I'm in love with this world, and with everything in it.

Thinking of my time outside, I recall the different view of my sculpture. I'd noticed for the first time it had company. Another large bronze just over and around the hill, out of my line of sight while I am in my room. Its style seemed dissimilar, more angular, and I realized as I shared the sun with them, my sculpture has a friend. I turned towards the sunlight and smiled. This new find proved to me my sculpture, my species and its creations, are social. They are meant to be given, shared, not restrained and hidden. The light is their natural element as well as ours, and I was finding meaning in the leaves and the grass, looking at my new, mysterious bronze friend.

Clarity of vision isn't enough. My telescope can show me the moon, but what of its dark side? We must be willing to change our perspective if we are to understand what we are. What we are capable of.

I've personified matter, imbued light and heat with emotions I can feel, and I laugh. I'm talking to birds and bronze, to bedpans and boxes of macaroni and cheese, and in spite of that I feel saner than I ever have in my life. The idea that doing so would appear odd to anyone seems quite wrong, and I'm again reminded in some ways I died the same day Hellen did. These personal revelations of change are starting to hurt less, and some of them, like this one, feel very good.

But I'm lucky, because I can still enjoy this day. This beautiful day I've created for myself.

I'll be leaving the hospital soon, and I'll need to work hard to make sure I can visit places like this every day.

I have so much to learn, and I've never been happier.

## 31 SEPTEMBER 17

It's been almost two weeks since I was outside, and the doctors are giving me the hairy eyeball. I know they want me out of this bed, to make room for their next medical mission. I'll be able to leave soon enough, but not all of me wants to.

Part of me is scared to death.

Physio went well yesterday and today, and I'm able to walk using those canes with the arm braces. Just a few unsupported steps between the parallel bars, but I'm getting more confident. Lacy says a walker would be better for me, but I feel like the mobility these canes offer is too much of an advantage. The extra effort to make them work is probably doing me good, anyway. I've found no matter how badly I feel I'm abusing my body, it seems to deal with it just fine. The ongoing pain isn't fun, that goes without saying, but the functions my body are supposed to take care of, like standing or walking, just seem to be something it understands. At least as long as I stay on top and give it those extra pushes from time to time.

My mind has been more restless of late. Markus tells me that's one of the surest signs a person is ready to go home, and I believe it. Since my arrival, I keep finding examples of relativity in my life, things like the greatest pain I've ever experienced being superseded, just a week later, by another even greater pain. That sort of thing. My boredom is starting to feel that way.

Every day has become an effort of endurance, not from the pain or the uncertainty of my future, but from the monotony of my environment. The sonic tedium of this ward, repeated precisely, once every twenty four hours.

I've been occupying myself by thinking about the world. Thinking about my views on it and my place in it. So much thought on affairs most people really don't give a moment to, at least not without an external prod. Even then, the public's attention isn't usually held for very long, not like this. I've been thinking for two months on my world, and I find these thoughts are going somewhere. I couldn't see it when I arrived, but my mind had a goal, and now that I'm getting close it's trying to make itself more clear. It demands action.

As I mentioned before, I'm feeling poetic, lyrical even, but I'm not just feeling a mood. I'm feeling an imperative. I am changed as a man, and I want to tell others, to share, to show, to make myself a public thing. I want the world to understand what I understand, what I think, and I imagine by doing this I'll make the world a better place.

Meanwhile, the television hangs ignored over my bed, unmoved by my endless little epiphanies.

I either have a huge ego or a huge psychosis. Perhaps they're the same thing.

Everyone has been so friendly to me; they've done as much as they could to make this time easier for me, each one of them, and in spite of that I feel like a boy about to tell a girl they shouldn't see each other any more.

I'm so tired of these walls. Tired of the tubes and of having my blood pressure taken four times a day. I'm tired of knowing my bowel movements are marked in a chart and tired of these drugs.

I am especially tired of the drugs.

The endless supply of morphine I'm so convinced is keeping me numb. I'll miss that the least when I go, in spite of my brain's often crushing desire to bring the morphine mistress home.

Thinking this, I have a moment of clarity and decide to act. I reach back over my shoulder and thumb the call button.

The long wait has once again begun, and today I'm going to give myself a goal. I'm going to cut myself off from the narcotics, and when I leave this place I'll be free from the fog forever. I can no longer hide the real world from myself, even if it's something as visceral as the pain my healing body feels it must provide me. I'm going to take that pain and wear it like a badge, and my scars will be my resume of strength, letting everyone know I'm able to live through things others might not.

The red light flashing above my head gives me a sense of deja-vu. I've been here before, and I begin to feel it in my stomach, that prescient sense of having done something of great import I'll do again soon. The feeling takes me by surprise and I feel unbalanced by it.

My head rests on my sterile pillow, and to calm my nerves I wonder about haircuts. I wonder about clothes. I wonder about underwear and shoes. I have a life, a real one, and although it exists only in my head, I'm going to make it real. My canes, my voice, we are going to drag the thing that will be my life out into the sun, the new clean air, and that will be the vehicle that carries me forward.

I'm feeling confident. Scared out of my mind, but confident. I've noticed that about making decisions. Good or bad, committing to a course of action and following through has got to be one of the greatest drugs a human can experience. My body is crippled and my emotions, my very self, destroyed and rebuilt, and yet here I am, feeling like a king. No room for doubts about my future. No place for doubts about my worth. In spite of my fears I'm becoming something greater than any religious follower ever could. I'm becoming self-realized, completely, and the world I inhabit is mine to fix.

No god will do this for me. I'll do it for the god, so that he may learn.

The crimson strobe pulses its anxious time into the space above my head, the insatiable clock of 4b, and as I notice it a nurse walks into the room. I can't remember her name, but she's always been nice to me. As usual, I sense that cool disconnection so many health care providers seem to have, but I'm feeling strong and committed. I get right to the point.

"I would like you to put an order on my file no more pain killers are to be provided to me, save for the after physio injections, and then only if I appear to truly need them. I'm not planning on having a discussion with my doctor about this as I've made up my mind. Please let him know if he has any objections, I plan on being quite stubborn this time. Also, is it possible to get a pad of writing paper and a pen?"

She dutifully reminds me that, having been on pain killers for so long, there will be a strong withdrawal reaction. If it is severe enough I might need treatment. I assure her I will not object to being helped if I have a bad reaction, but I'm counting on them to use their judgement. I need to end this dependence my way.

"I'll let the doctor know what you want. I'm sure he'll have no objections," she says. Her eyes are smiling.

I feel her humanity, the cool facade replaced by warmth, and I take strength in this new connection as she assures me they'll do whatever they can to help me through this. Her hope and her words comfort me, and I brace myself against what I know is coming. Soon I'll feel the fractured hand of addiction as it secures its grip on my throat. Tighter and more desperate this time because it knows, it is certain, this will be its last chance.

I'm going to kill another god, and this god is going to try and stop me.

## SEPTEMBER 17, NIGHT — 32

"We are a people company."

The fluorescent lighting sends a quiet buzz into the room, and I'm sitting in front of an expensive looking coffee table. A selection of digital readers are displayed in front of me, and out of curiosity I pick one up and scan the menu. A good assortment of books have already been downloaded onto the device, and with a few button presses I see it's connected to an account. I can get whatever book or magazine I want, just a quick download away.

I'm in a waiting room, a large foyer actually, and it is starkly corporate in its design. The walls are an orange colour, or at least they rest somewhere in that part of the spectrum, and the hue is so subtle you could be forgiven for not realizing it was actually orange. The seat I'm occupying is black leather (what else is there?) and the arm rests are thick and padded, with lots of room between the chairs.

No sense having the alphas fighting in the lobby while they are waiting to do business.

The lighting is indirect. The floors expensive and neutral. Even the desk is a stereotype. Shoulder high in the front, with all the metallic and wooden accents required to make the standard corporate submission-inspiring first impression.

If you are being made to wait in this room, chances are good you're not very important to the company, but they most certainly don't want you to think so. These fixtures come from the most expensive stores and they speak to those who use them in subtle tones, making subtle suggestions:

Sit back. Relax. You are in the presence of majesty and greatness, and soon it will be your turn. Be happy.

On the wall above the desk, thick silver lettering reminds you 'We are a people company.'

"I guess they want me to know they like people," I think to myself sarcastically.

I imagine the message is supposed to be much deeper than my sardonic response would imply. Much more meaningful. Considering they paid well over seven-million-dollars to research and implement that tagline, I should hope it has some depth.

I don't know how I know that.

I'm here for an interview, appropriately five minutes early. I've been packaged in an expensive suit Hellen must have picked out, and it makes me feel a bit uneasy. She always buys me shirts with collars that are too tight, and I spend my time trying not to pass out from lack of blood to the brain. She suggested this company might be a good fit for me, considering my newfound desire to celebrate humanity. To celebrate people.

"They are a people company," she told me as I dressed.

Returning my attention to the digital reader, I settle on a work by Mark Twain. I've read it dozens of times; I skip ahead to one of my favourite chapters and settle in.

Immediately I notice something isn't right. As I read the familiar text there are references being made to this company, and I'm certain they never existed that long ago. As I continue to read of Mark Twain's travels in the middle east, I arrive at a scene where a guide, familiar to me from so many prior readings, turns to him and states in a hushed tone:

"They are a people company."

I know the story, and his character never said that.

My confusion is interrupted by the sound of a door opening. I replace the reader back among its counterparts on the table and put on my best job interview face. Through the door comes an unexpected apparition. An angel. A real one with wings and a halo and beautiful flowing whites robes. As the door closes silently behind him he glides towards me, his intent to arrive apparently his only motivating force. No part of him touches the ground. He stops before me, towering over my head, and I realize I'm face-to-face with an angel. His wings continue to beat in a slow cadence as he hovers, effortlessly. The effect is hypnotic, and it is clear to me his wings were never meant to be used for anything as mundane as mere flight, but instead their purpose is ornamental. He is beautiful, and I'm in awe in a way I've never experienced before.

He offers me his hand.

"Hello," he begins, "you must be the new recruit. Welcome."

My heart trips in my chest.

It seems being an angel is the norm here, and judging from his demeanour he certainly isn't expecting a fuss, so I react in a way I hope is not too casual or too effusive. I solemnly take the angel's hand as offered and give it three good shakes, just as Hellen advised. I'm still quite speechless, and so I'm relieved when he simply nods his head to acknowledge the exchange. Without further ceremony he turns back towards the already opening door, his flowing robes the only indication of motion I can detect. I follow automatically.

"Before we get to the interview stage I want to offer you a tour of our factory floor. Our applicants don't often realize just how pervasive, how ubiquitous, our products are." I notice as he speaks my feet leave the ground, and before I have time to register the novelty of the situation, I find myself levitating next to him, without wings, simply willing myself in the direction I want to go.

What a very pleasant feeling.

We make our way down a long corridor, and as his presence fills me with a strong sense of well-being, I notice a name on the front of his glowing robe, embroidered directly into the weave of his tunic. I can see my angel's name is Emmanuel.

"Just call me Manny."

Part of me understands he did not speak the words.

As I float next to him, Manny begins to tell me about the company. He boasts they are the number one supplier of durable goods to 'this and that' retail chain, and the names on his list are all very familiar. I'm quite impressed, and in spite of my desire to remain calm for the interview, I decide a bit of enthusiasm is probably a good thing. Who wants a disinterested employee? I offer polite and positive responses, exactly as Hellen taught me.

I am perfect.

We move down the hallway for what seems like a long time. All I can see are industrial lighting and cleanliness. The walls are devoid of markings. Finally, I see a door in the distance, and when we arrive he ushers me through. I move quickly into the room, and just for effect I decide to spin upwards a few dozen feet. The view is spectacular and in front of me lays a vista that is difficult to describe. We have entered a room, but the room is the world. As far as I can see there are rows of small desks, each one with an employee standing or sitting near it. They are all working, all busy, and the atmosphere is one of a hive. I can actually feel the buzz of humans, their chatter and their beating hearts, moving the air and the world from this impossibly large space.

Manny watches me silently as I survey his company's creation. From my vantage point I can see a long line of people waiting at each desk. They have that uncomfortable look of men waiting for a urinal, shuffling from one foot to the other, anxious for their turn. They are all watching the person working the desk with apprehension, and I'm curious why. Thousands upon thousands of desks, most probably in the millions, and at each desk is a worker being furtively watched.

Very curious.

I notice Manny is starting to glow even more luminously, something I wouldn't have thought possible, and I watch as he rises higher and higher. I follow him, and the view is amazingly clear. I can see for hundreds of miles, the desks clearly number in the millions, and each one with its occupant and a line.

My angel rises higher still, and as he does his colour starts to change. Slowly, imperceptibly, his colour shifts until eventually he shines a brilliant blue. Looking down, I can see his blue light illuminating the entire area, the thousands of miles and the millions of desks, all starting to reflect in deference to Manny's aura. We continue to rise, and I can feel the air thinning in my chest. I close my eyes and see his face in my soul. His former gentle glow has become such a scorching blue radiance I can no longer look directly at him. He is the only light anywhere.

Manny and I, so impossibly high, look down at the men and women below us. I can see the bright blue cast has drained the colour from their faces.

I look towards Manny squinting, shading my face, and he turns to me, his eyes fiery and wide, and tells me I don't understand. "But you will ... here comes the good part. Pay attention, because we are about to make this quarter. This will put us over the top!"

His words have an edge to them, a blade-on-blade feeling of certainty, and I'm suddenly very afraid.

Looking down on the shop floor, on the entire world, I can see his staff working endlessly, and as I watch them Manny changes colour again.

An explosive blast of air momentarily pushes me from my place by his side, and now he is red - hard, dark, blood-red; his eyes look straight down. Wings and arms spread wide, he licks his lips, his new blood-red reptilian lips, and I watch as the first person in each line begins to walk towards their desk.

The operators remain oblivious. They've kept up their pace, increased it if anything, and I notice the millions of people walking towards the desks are each dressed exactly the same as the people working them. As they arrive they pick up some sort of cylindrical tool. It's attached to the desk by a long black tube, and they hold it as casually as I would hold a pen.

Then stillness. They have all arrived.

Standing.

Waiting.

During the pause I look at their faces and I can see they are happy. Their looks of joy are as plain as the burning red light being broadcast by Manny.

Satisfied, his eyes narrow slightly, and I can feel something is about to happen. His wings spread even wider. His head falls back. The look on his face is almost orgasmic in its pure lusting pleasure.

This is clearly Manny's favourite part.

"Now."

The millions of men and women who were first in line step forward, calmly pressing the business-end of their mysterious instrument against the heads of the employees still busy working the desk. Most of the workers don't even notice as the cold pressure of the device pushes them forward, save for a few, and they do little more than make quick yelping noises as the bolt crashes through their skulls and deep into their brains.

The bodies of the workers fall to the floor, landing in unison - synchronized, poetic and terminal. I can see thick blood, ghoulish and white in this red light, as it sprays through the holes in their destroyed skulls. Two, three, sometimes four thick ejaculations splash onto the floor next to them before it stops.

Manny's eyes are wide and eager.

"Watch and learn how it's done," he growls to me softly. I feel the skin on my face starting to burn.

As he speaks, I can see the desks are opening up, all of them, and as they do, large mechanical claws emerge from within. The changed desks reach for the dead bodies and lift them, grappling and positioning them. As they do, the clothing is carefully removed, and as it comes off, yet more tools emerge, transforming the cloth into products I recognize.

I see a scarf, much like the one I bought for Hellen last Christmas.

Endless pairs of socks.

Underwear.

The desk machines move quickly. Arms and legs are removed as fast as I can follow, and they're moulded and shaped into dishes, bicycles, coffee makers. The efficiency of the machines is horrific, and my rational mind is devastated as I watch the evidence of their intelligent design. Even the pooled and dripping blood is being gathered by articulated suctioning tubes, transformed into bottled water and sparkling soft drinks.

All that remains of the butchered humans is a head and a torso, and I'm hardly able to control my fear as the desks reach up and slam two large metal plates together, crushing the skulls. The plates stay in place for a moment, and then with a noise that causes me to loose control of my voice, they wrest the gruesome mess off the necks. Scraping and grinding, horrible soul-killing sounds. They worry the head-meat back and forth until the metal plates move mechanically to one side and open over clean trays. From the pristine steel comes millions of laptop computers and smart phones.

I'm yelling. Begging. I'm demanding Manny explain this horrific display, and his response is laughter at my distress. His laughter tears at my suit, leaving welts on my skin.

The naked remains are manoeuvred into large openings on the

desktops, and millions of lids slide closed, taking them temporarily from my sight. My reprieve does not last long, and in just a few seconds I weep as they open, the sterile silver trays rising like synchronized offerings. On them are various cuts of meat, packaged and labelled, ready for shipping.

It's done. There's nothing left of them.

"Damn. That was a good quarter."

Manny's colour shifts back to white, and I can see below me the room, the world, is also returning to its original state. The person who had been first in line is happily working the desk, doing whatever it is the desk machine asks of them, and behind them stands the rest of the line. The people waiting at the front are still shifting and shuffling their feet, all of them anxious to get their turns.

What I feel is beyond emotion. Beyond rage. I yell at Manny with such profound anger, I know if he gives me the slightest chance I'll kill him.

"How can you expect me to work here, when you show me this is how you treat your employees! You sick fuck! You killed them all! You're killing the whole fucking world!"

My breath is coming hard and sharp in my chest, the lack of oxygen at this altitude is making me dizzy, and I can feel a primal madness taking charge.

His eyes shift to look at me, directly into me, and Manny lets out a huge laugh. Its force makes me cower, hovering crumpled and burning in the air next to him. The world below feels his appreciation of my innocence, and through my terror I see many of the people working the desks looking up, trying to see what is amusing their angel so much.

"Employees? We are one of the most profitable pan-national corporations on earth. Those aren't employees ... they're customers."

He speaks the words through the widest smile I've ever seen.

I feel the idea settle into my consciousness, violating it, and then I understand.

"We are a people company!"

## SEPTEMBER 18, EVENING — 33

It's impossible to sleep when your bones are fighting.

I keep telling myself I'm going to make it. This is going to happen.

I grit my teeth as the feelings tear their way through me. I'm entirely unable to control my emotions, and when I'm not asleep I spend hours at a time crying. Sobbing and wailing and weeping, the prostrate victim of chemistry, my raw emotions on display.

I thought the rising sun was going to kill me. For the first time in weeks I asked the nurses to close the drapes, and although the darkness improved things, it wasn't enough. I could feel the heat of the fall sun coming through the plastic blinds, through the walls. Eventually I had to throw off my blanket and my clothes - anything to cool off.

It's been a bit more than a day since my morphine was cut and it's been worse than I thought. Far worse. I'm trying to ignore it but my brain wants to leave my head, and I'm fighting the urge to pound it back in with the bedpan. My legs are so heavy I need to haul them by hand from place to place on my bed, and trying to eat anything but ice cream has been a disaster.

Ginger ale and vanilla ice cream.

All night long, one after the other. Vanilla ice cream and ginger ale. They kept bringing it and I kept taking it. They didn't try to stop me because they said sugar and liquids would help.

Fucking drugs would help me too.

I can't find my bedding, and I'm so cold. My sheet and blanket seem to be missing. Someone had better get their act together around here, a guy can't be expected to get through the sort of crap I've experienced without a blanket.

What kind of two-bit operation has no blankets?

I hug myself. My stomach hurts and I want to keep the panic away. I can feel the bones under my skin. I need to stay on top of this thing. I'm finding it hard to control my emotions, so hard, and they don't even have anything to keep me warm.

I look at the shaded window and I know Soleil and my sculpture are outside, waiting for me. I know they are; I can hear them, but the bird is telling me to hurry up. Someone is in the park. It's the priests, and they've brought tools. I hear screaming as they start to saw at the base of my sculpture. I try to stand, I have to get out of bed and save my friend, but I'm unable to support my weight and I fall on the floor. Just a cold wet mess someone will need to clean.

I can see my blanket.

What kind of a two-bit operation keeps bedding under the bed? This is just not fucking acceptable, and it's a good thing it's so hot down here, or I would be mighty pissed. Mighty fucking pissed indeed.

My leg hurts.

I ask my dad what he suggests for this sort of thing, and he says dealers who wear loafers have the best drugs because they sell to the corporate types. Lawyers don't waste their time buying crap from hoods, and so he tells me to look for a dealer wearing loafers.

Before I do I should probably get my blanket. It's freezing in here.

I notice some light on the floor from the window, just a sliver, and I watch it slowly advance across the room. I retreat under my bed. The priests must have sent it after me, and I can see it's not a lot, but it will be enough. I hope it can't reach me under here because I know I won't be able to escape. I look into my future, and I can see myself alone in the dark room as the light finds me. It sparks into a flame and I'm consumed.

I really don't want that to happen.

I'm so hot, but I cover myself with my blanket, and I look out from my fortress to see if I can get out. My leg aches, it's really hard to think, and if I could just stop the priests from hurting my friend I would be alright.

I can see loafers.

I see them walking into the room and pausing. Am I supposed to pay them? Should I make some sort of secret sound so they know I'm buying? When I was a teenager the dealers downtown used to whisper hash under their breath, so I try it.

"HASH!"

I think that was louder than I meant. The loafers got the point though, and they are coming towards me.

In my fortress I wait for the man who will save me from my bones. I tried, I really tried, but it's just too fucking cold to wait around for them to stop this shit on their own.

"Nurse! Nurse! Page Dr. Calm for bed 4b!"

The loafers are looking under the bed, but that's my doctor, and I realize it's a sting and I'm getting busted.

"FUCK! FUCK!"

The doctor reaches under the bed for my arm, my good arm, and my legs hurt so much I can't think. A women arrives and I can see she is carrying a needle. Oh man, I hope it's the needle I want.

The floor is smooth and the sliver of light is afraid of my doctor, so I don't burst into flames when it hits me, but I can feel it trying to get into my head and I can see blood on the floor - my friend's blood. The priests got him. My sculpture is dead.

What will I do?

The doctor and the nurse pick me up off the floor and return me to my bed. The two railings on either side of the bed are raised, and I hear the doctor ask about doses. He looks me right in the eye. I'm so afraid, I wish they would help my friend.

"You've cut yourself, so we're going to bandage you and give you a sedative. You should be able to sleep for a while," my doctor says.

They don't understand. That's not my blood; it's my friend's. I'm so sad for him, alone in the park, so beautiful, and they killed him. He was so innocent. Why did they kill him?

I'm crying quietly as they bandage my foot and inject the sedative.

"Keep those railings up until he is through this. I can't believe they weren't already in place."

"Sorry doctor."

I open my eyes. The light has moved. It's on the wall, and I know it can't get me up there. I don't see the doctor or the nurse, and I know I'll get through this. Just have to hold on.

It's not going to be easy in this room. It's always so fucking cold.

# 34 SEPTEMBER 22, EARLY MORNING

The nurse makes sure the patient is sleeping, then sits down to examine his chart.

She rarely has a chance to get to know her patients well, but he has been here quite a while, and she's enjoyed his company. He's been making good progress lately, and the unprofessional human part of her will miss him, but unless complications hold him up, he'll be leaving soon. Probably in less than a week if homecare can be arranged.

His vitals are all perfectly normal.

She thinks to herself this guy has a heart like a piston, and for his sake she's glad the withdrawal should be finishing soon. He's had a tough time. Some patients endure the withdrawal at home, which is supposed to be less scary, but normally they go through it here in the hospital. They are weaned off the meds slowly, less traumatically.

He insisted on cold turkey though.

Some do.

She lifts his arm to take his blood pressure and gets a groan from him. He's an active sleeper, and she can see he's in the middle of a dream. His eyes are moving quickly back and forth beneath the lids.

"You just dream the nasty stuff away and I'll take care of everything else. With any luck you won't remember any of it," she says.

He has water in the plastic carafe, a cup and a bendy straw, two small bottles of ginger ale, and his crutches are leaning against the wall by his head. She knows he will be walking without assistance soon, and she silently wishes him well. Most patients have some help when they leave, most often family, sometimes friends, but he's alone. Twice a day homecare visits will be all he has, so he'll have a lot of adjusting to do. Nobody is ever truly prepared to face their familiar home with the challenges of unfamiliar disabilities, but he can take comfort knowing the effects of his injuries will eventually fade. In time he should make a full recovery.

Opening the blinds, new light fills the room. The effect satisfies her. Natural lighting is good for the mood and he's always insisted on leaving the window open.

Looking out, she can see it's going to be a memorable fall day. The sun is bright, the leaves are stunning in their autumn colours, and the park is already full of people enjoying what could be the last grassy walk of the year.

We don't usually get snow this early, but it has been known to happen, she thinks.

As she makes her way to the door, she looks back on the room to make sure she isn't forgetting anything. She notices how thin he's become. A quick note in his chart suggesting an increase in caloric intake makes her fell better.

He was a big guy when he got here and she's concerned.

"Dr. Hamilton likes to prescribe Guinness to patients when they leave. Hope you like dark beer," she says through a grin.

Kit in hand, she softly closes the door behind her.

## SEPTEMBER 22, LATE MORNING 35

I am awake, and as I'm drawn evermore into the conscious world I can already sense something is different.

I smell better.

My eyes are really sore, so I squint. The light seems too bright, and my head is aching in a way I know sunlight won't help. It seems to be morning, probably around ten I would guess. Through my delicate vision I notice a couple of small bottles of ginger ale on my table. One of them appears to have been opened to allow it to go flat.

That would be good; I'm really thirsty.

I pour myself a small cupful, my hands dry and thick, and I have a cautious drink. The effect on me is instant, and after a couple of sips I feel better. I had forgotten how it can soothe.

I'm back home as a child, mom giving me little plastic cups of flat ginger ale to calm my upset stomach.

I try to recall what's been going on and all that comes to me is the feeling, the certainty actually, things were odd for a while. I can tell time has passed, perhaps as much as a couple of days, but it's hard to say as my memory feels weird. It's as if the last little while has all been a dream.

I suppose in one sense it was.

I pry my eyes open a bit more and they slowly allow the light in. Stretching my vision, I can see the park and my sculpture are shiny and clean, and I remember it is fall. My sculpture is wet, and I initially think it must be from condensation or rain, but then I see someone is there with a hose and a brush, cleaning it. As I watch them gather their things to leave I remember my dream, the one where someone was removing the sculpture, and my fear for its safety briefly returns. I get a chill.

Dreams can be crazy things. So real, so vivid, and so irrational.

I enjoy the idea the sculpture is getting cleaned, and it occurs to me I've never seen a sculpture cleaned. Is it a normal thing to do? I would think so, but I have to admit I've never heard of it before.

The room is silent and still. If I tried, I could probably hear my own heart beating, and the silence is making me think it must be earlier than ten. I wonder if breakfast has been around.

The unexpected thought of food causes my mind to jump. I'm thinking of bacon and eggs, and immediately I have to stifle a gag. The idea of fat and grease repulses me, and my stomach rebels at the merest thought of them.

I hold my hand to my mouth as I wait for the feeling to pass.

As my queasiness begins to fade, I realize I really do smell better. That disgusting alien odour that caused me so much discomfort is almost gone. I think with a few showers using real soap, I could get it off of me completely. Of course, just the idea of standing for any amount of time is asking a bit much, never mind doing it while standing in hot, soapy water. I really miss that lost sense of luxurious comfort. Then I think of the fall I had in physio and I let the idea leave my head. The first thirty seconds or so might be great, but after that?

Healing is hard work - showers will come later.

I wonder if I'm well enough to go to physio today? I don't remember having gone for a while, and a shower is as good a motivator as anything else I can think of. I can see my box of macaroni and cheese sitting on the bed by my feet, and judging from the wear on the corners it could probably use a shower as well.

The joke makes me smile.

My eyes are getting used to the light, and I try again to remember what's been going on the last little while. I can recall chunks of dreams, mostly quite scary ones, and not a lot more. Whatever happened to me seems to be gone with the fog, the chemical mist dispersed, taking my memory with it. As I work to bring back the time, I find the sensation of personal loss growing more and more acute. The idea things have happened I can't recall, emotions and thoughts and ideas simply gone, forces me to wonder, how much of myself have I lost?

How much of me was the morphine, and how much was just me?

I'm paranoid I'm no longer myself. What an unsettling feeling.

A deep breath, and I try to change the page. I allow myself to notice how my body feels different. The pain is still there, but that's not very surprising. When haven't I been strained by some sort of pain since I arrived? It's different though. I feel like my limbs are more connected to me. More mine. I try to move my legs and they respond differently. They feel heavy, exhausted, but when I tell them to move, the signal is clearly more substantial. I try tensing up my legs and my buttocks, and the feeling is encouraging. No sharp pains make me want to stop, just that deep, dull ache of healing.

They feel better. I'm definitely coming out the other side of this withdrawal.

A dream comes back to me with force. A dream about corporations. It was a bad one, and I remember the helpless sense of panic it left within me.

The idea behind corporations has always bothered me; they are the ultimate enablers of the cash god's crimes, after all, and when facing the God of Cash in these foggy mental debates I shouldn't be too surprised when it turns up in my sleep, forcing me to watch the harvest.

I guess getting off the meds hasn't changed me as much as I feared. Here I am, hardly awake and right back at it.

As I ponder the universe, and the flaws we've added to it, Markus enters the room. His first glance tells me he wasn't expecting to see me awake, but as soon as he realizes I'm up he starts right in.

"Are you back? Think you might be up for a walk in the gym?"

"I feel good. Yeah, I think I am. Is there anything around to eat? Something light?" I ask.

"I'll find you some crackers, anything else will probably make you sick. As for the walk, I'll see if I can get Lacy to find a spot for you in the gym for this afternoon. That sound ok?"

"Sounds great," I reply. I had been thinking about him and Lacy, and my curiosity gets the better of me. I ask about their relationship.

"Markus, you don't have to answer if this is too personal, but are you and Lacy married?" As I wait for his reply, I'm worried I might have crossed some unwritten boundary, but Markus doesn't even flinch. I feel better.

"Oh yeah we're married. Extremely married. It's probably been about seven years. How could you tell?"

Could I tell him it was because of how he looked at her? My leering gorilla, stalking the female in the sterile, green-walled jungle of the hospital? I decided to be polite, but truthfully.

"How you look at each other. It seemed obvious after I noticed it."

"Makes sense, I guess. I thought you noticed the tattoos," he responded.

"Tattoos?"

"Our tattoos. We got them when we were married, as a sort of remembrance of how we met," he explained. He lifted the cuff of his right leg, and there on his calf muscle was a perfect match to the telescope tattoo I had seen on Lacy.

"Interesting." A story hidden behind matching tattoos.

Markus continues with the bureaucratic medical routine of my biology.

"You've been getting a sedative these last few days, but I don't think you'll need them anymore. You good with that?"

I hadn't realized I had been on any, so I told him no, I wouldn't be needing any more. If the drugs still left in my body have anything else to say, I'm sure at this point I can handle it.

I watch Markus make another note on my chart.

Heart rate and blood pressure checked and noted, Markus is getting ready to leave when he turns and casually asks me an unexpected question.

"How about you? Married?"

Without thought I'm about to answer him, but the mental reflex is derailed, and I feel a sharp stab of emotion as I realize for the first time in years I have to answer ... no. Immediately, I feel tears on my cheeks. The quiet morning sunlight is the only joy left in the room, and my voice drops in volume as I begin to explain.

"I was married. Her name was Hellen, but she died in the crash that brought me here. We were separated, but we were hoping to get back together."

Markus looks surprised. "Hellen Bergstrohm? That was your wife?"

I tell him yes, and ask him how he knew her maiden name. When we were married she had taken mine.

Markus explains. "The news story about her accident. They said she was with an acquaintance when the accident happened. They went on for a long time about her job and her family. I'm so sorry to have brought it up."

An acquaintance.

I realized what happened right away. Her family, even then, even when dealing with the tragic and unexpected death of one of their own, was working to create a legal distance between myself and Hellen's money. Clearly, they expect an attempt from me to claim some of their family wealth. If I checked I would probably find someone in the local media either works for them, or even more likely, they simply own a portion of the local news desk outright.

I hold my breath. They are wasting their time. As far as I'm concerned they can keep their money. I want nothing to do with it.

I exhale frustration into the room.

For the hundredth time since I arrived I find myself angry at Hellen. What sort of vulture did she think I was? Because of her wealth we even signed a prenuptial agreement, and yet her family still tries to separate us, even after her death? Was this something she had written into her will when we separated?

Stop ... exhale.

I let the thoughts go, breathing them into the room, into the universe, knowing they are not going to take me anywhere good. I'm almost out of this hospital, this morgue for the soul, and the last thing I need is another reason to brood.

My new found atheist convictions are more than enough to keep me busy, thanks.

My eyes are wet and red, and as I wipe them dry I can see Markus hasn't left. He seems to be waiting for something, so I ask him what it might be. Markus seems unsure how to proceed.

"Well," he begins, "Lacy and I have spoken about that accident. A couple of times actually, and please forgive me if I'm sounding forward or putting my nose where it doesn't belong, but that accident ... it wasn't really an accident, was it?"

There it is. The question never given voice, and a part of me is a bit surprised to be hearing it. I assumed no-one knew what had happened that night. The fact no police have ever questioned me in all the time I've been here made me certain it was considered open and shut. Can I tell him what happened? Can I tell this man, my gorilla nurse, how my wife tried to kill us?

I falter.

"Markus, I really like you, but I'm not ready. I can't. After I'm home, after I have Franklin on my lap and the world is spinning in the right direction again, then I would love for you and Lacy to visit, and I'll tell you what I remember. But not today. Not now."

He nods. He understands.

Twice in just a few minutes I'm feeling choked up with emotion, and I'm wondering if I'll be forever-plagued with this hair-trigger weeping. I hope not. I try to casually wipe my face again, to remove the second accumulation of tears. As if reading my mind, Markus assures me emotions tend to be closer to the surface for patients, especially after going through a tough withdrawal, and I should try not to worry about it.

"After they go home, most patients tend to find their base pretty quickly, and the strength they remember returns. It'll happen that way for you too. I'm sorry I upset you."

"Thanks Markus, you've been a good friend."

"No problem, anytime. I am curious though, who is Franklin?"

# 36

SEPTEMBER 22, EVENING

Back from physio and I've just had a visit from the doctor. It seems I'll probably be going home in two days. Homecare has been arranged, the medical equipment I'll need to make my condo work for me while I convalesce has been ordered, and all that remains is for me to show them I can walk twenty feet without the parallel bars and I can go.

Two days. I'm not ready.

I want to leave. I really do, but two days? I can barely make my way from the bed to the wheelchair for physio, how am I supposed to live a life on my own? How am I suppose to feed Franklin?

I look out my window at the warmth of autumn. The colours are talking to me, trying to calm me, they are so beautiful. I really am feeling more emotional, and my eyes water just a bit as I imagine arriving home. I can see myself walking in the door and finding

Franklin.

He will be the first familiar face I've seen in the many weeks, the months, I've been away.

Just two days.

I crack open a ginger ale and drink from the little bottle, and I can almost hear myself asking the bartender for another. The fizzy drink and my window are familiar and comfortable, and I settle myself deeper into my bed to wait for the sunset.

I'll be fine.

Homecare is apparently going to help me do meal prep, and I'm sure if I asked them they could give a cat a few kibbles. They are even going to do things like laundry for me, so the hardest thing I'm likely to have to deal with will be making sure I don't go nuts from boredom. Then I remember asking for a pen and some paper, all those days ago.

Is it here? Did they bring it?

I sit up in bed, the muscles of my back still tired from physio, and I lean over to the dresser next to my bed. I've never tried to get anything out of the drawers before, so I reach over not sure how it will go. My hand grasps the handle and I pull. The drawer opens without complaint. Leaning further, I see paper, but I don't see a pen. I lean over a bit further, and with great care and grace, I fall.

The pain is worse because I wasn't expecting it.

I've fallen half-off the bed. My hands are palms down and flat on the floor, while my arms are straight and angry, holding me up. My bad arm is already starting to howl. The blood is flowing down into my still-mangled hand, and that horrible swelling, that feeling of painful pressure, is all I can think of. If I don't get myself back into bed soon my arm will fail. I'll fall. I can't push myself back into bed, so I have to get my legs down.

How are my legs going to take that landing?

I call out, but even if someone hears me, can they arrive in time? My body is slowly slipping off the bed, and I know this is it, I'm going to be hurt. My whole body is sweating already, and I can feel my hands getting slick from it. My legs slide further off the bed and my injured hand slides an inch further away from me.

Then it happens. My first leg slides over the edge, off the bed, and my foot touches down, toes splayed, supporting me. I'm not hurt. Somehow my reflexes saved me. Without thought to pain, my knee simply bent, and my leg caught me. Just as it would have had I not been hurt.

My hand slips further away from me on the floor, my sweaty palm unable to support my entire weight any longer, but I'm able to steady myself with my leg. I'm still not happy with this position; I'm still in trouble, but as I call out for help I slowly allow my other leg to leave the bed. I can't wait. The pain is too much. I need to get in control of this fall, and that's the only way it will happen.

I'm astonished a second time as my leg leaves the bed and touches down, harder and more painfully than I had hoped, but still toe to floor. Still safe.

On all fours, on the floor next to bed 4b, I allow myself to sink down. Slowly I turn onto my back, taking the pressure off of my arm. Bringing my hand and arm to my chest, I hold them over my heart waiting for some of the pain recede. All I can imagine is broken glass. I straighten my legs and that brings its own pains, so I rest on the floor as I plot my strategy.

Can I get back into bed on my own?

My muscles are so weak - another side effect of withdrawal according to the doctor, and after today's efforts in the gym I can't imagine I have the strength to do it.

I listen to the ward. Nobody is coming. I start up.

The bed rails are down and they are very secure, so I grab the bottom rung and pull. My body moves upwards just enough to make me think this will work. My goal is to get myself turned around so I'm on all fours again, then use the bed rails to pull myself up.

I pull again and now I'm mostly sitting, my shoulder to the bed and my legs splayed out in front of me. I notice they look more like a normal set of skinny legs, as long as I ignore the bruising and bandages. I pull them together and twist my upper body. The scar on my hip is awake and vocal as I turn myself onto my stomach. Supported by my elbows, exhaustion and nausea slow me down, but this is progress.

I breathe deeply, to settle my pains and calm myself.

Feeling confident, I press my arms out in front of me and push my backside up. The pain comes back, familiar and expected, as I walk my hands backwards. In a moment I find myself on all fours again, facing my bed, and really thinking I'll be able to do this.

I look at my pain, a spectator at a brawl, and I can see it rolling back and forth over me. It's so large I imagine it deserves a sound track, something catchy but serious, and I start to hum little themes I think might be appropriate.

My smell brings me back.

I'm sweating hard, and that hospital smell I hate so much is in there with it. My hands are all moisture and pain, my scars stretched as they slide on the floor, and I realize I had better finish this or I'll be defeated by the sheer slickness I'm creating.

Reaching up, I get one hand on the rail, then the other. The fingers of my scarred hand close hard on the rail, and through the pain I can feel I have a good grip.

I pull myself towards the bed.

Hand-over-hand I climb, my head filled with the smell of panic and sweat, and more quickly than I would have thought possible, I'm vertical. My body presses tightly to the bed rail, while my poor knees yell for relief from the hard hospital floor. They haven't supported my entire weight since before the accident, and I feel tears forming as the pain takes me. This has to stop.

Keep going. Not too long now.

One foot. I need to get one foot under me to push with. I'm right handed, so I chose the right foot. I imagine it must be stronger. As I pull my right leg up more weight is applied to my left knee. My poor, damaged, bruised, left knee. The pain is beyond scary, and I'm questioning my ability to do this. I have to stop. I have to lay down. My leg keeps coming though, and with a final desperate effort I feel my right foot settle onto the floor in a position that can hold weight.

No time to wait, the pain is just too much, and I push with my right leg. My shattered and atrophied muscles try to support my frame, this skeletal satire, and the shaking is almost comical.

Anyone witnessing this could be forgiven for thinking I was faking it.

I keep pressing and the muscles keep trying, and I can feel my knee leave the floor. The pain changes, and I'm watching dispossessed as my left leg starts to straighten. My arms are pulling me up and the sweat on my face is making my eyes burn, and through it I can see my legs are almost there, almost together. My left foot finds its place, and with an unsettling sense of vertigo I realize I'm standing next to my bed without any walking aids.

I'm standing next to my bed.

I look at my hands and I tell them to let go. They do. My hands fall gently to my side, and for the first time since Hellen tried to kill me, I'm standing without help.

The tears are back and I can't tell them from the sweat. My hospital gown has left me naked and exposed. The thin wet cloth is giving me a chill, and I remember why I'm here.

I gently turn myself to the partially opened drawer, and from my new vantage point I can see a pen. Blinking through the salt in my eyes, I stare for a moment at its efficient shape - the unadorned stretch of the barrel.

I'm in so much pain and I feel a deep love for my new pen.

Can I do this?

As deliberately as a man defusing a bomb, my hand reaches out and grasps the bed rail again. I take a small step and once again I can think only of broken glass. Another step, and another, and I'm over the drawer reaching down to grasp the pad of paper. I lift it slowly, its weight more than I expected, and place it on my bedside table. I reach for the pen; this troubling pen, and place it reverently on the paper.

I'm left standing next to the bed, sweating, scared, and feeling better than I have in days.

Weeks.

Years.

My mission accomplished, I feel my exhaustion more intimately. I don't think I can spin myself around to get onto the bed in any sort of normal way, so instead I lower myself face first onto the mattress and pull my legs up after me. Some painful adjusting, and I'm in bed, comfortable, but breathing as if I had just run a marathon.

I might as well have, I feel so good. Even my pain feels good.

Pen and paper on the bedside table and I need to get to work. I've been doing a lot of thinking, and I want to get it down. I want it all there, before I go home.

In two days.

# MY ATHEIST BIBLE 37

To write I have to sit up, my back almost vertical. My legs hurt from the strain, and my neck and shoulders ache ... but I work. The light from the window and the sound of the ward become invisible allies as I document my thoughts. I work through the discomfort. Time is expressed in meals; in trays deposited and removed. The notes are the only thing I care about.

I am consumed by the foolishness that is my dream, trying to express itself in ink.

*This is the beginning.*

*There was once a time when atheism was the default world view of all humans. Theism didn't exist, so its eventual opposite, a-theism, also didn't exist. We were born, lived, grew old and died, never once looking skyward for guidance or direction. We survived happily for millenia without religion. However, once we invented gods, things changed. We became selective in our application of rational thought and we suffered for it. It is my hope we atheists can return the species to that first, more lucid state. To render the term atheist obsolete, and by doing so, move human society forward.*

*We are a beautiful species. Unfettered, we spend our lives working to improve ourselves, growing constantly beyond our limitations to achieve more. We have accomplished the impossible countless times and one could be forgiven to think there is nothing beyond our reach. Look to our history. Each generation's impossible dream becomes the next generation's everyday reality.*

*It is time to attempt the impossible once again. It is time to rid our species of the gods.*

*How?*

*An atheist bible asks only that you embrace rationality and serve the good of humanity.*

*Religion will tell you it serves this purpose but its nature is tribal and exclusionary, and in today's world it is no longer enough. The world is shrinking. We are armed with weapons our ancestors could never have imagined. Our crowded planet is currently witnessing religious wars so acrimonious the downfall of our species appears inevitable. Our weapons are devastating, and the religious warriors wielding them are showing no restraint. Among the masses who worship, religion has become the primary means of identifying who should be subdued, who should be silenced, and who should be killed.*

*We are being consumed by the worshippers of Bronze-Age gods,* and for every body that falls in conflict, the God of Cash profits. It's assimilating as many of the old religions it can find, and wars that began as ideological debates are purposely being made to evolve into wars over land and resources. Guns and bombs, starvation and rape, killing believer and non-believer alike, and all of it to benefit the owners of the markets.

To survive, to do this impossible thing, a new way of seeing ourselves must evolve. I believe it already has.

There are self-actualizing men and women who exist, not to serve a god, but instead to serve their innate sense of self-improvement. They live on every continent, in every culture, in every social and economic class, doing every job we have devised. In many nations they are thought to be the majority, but in spite of that, they remain silent.

This must change. It is time to say goodbye to the intellectual crutches we've relied on for millenia, and insist the unthinking pious who would destroy us do the same.

To do so, we must understand the nature of our gods has changed. The avarice of the greatest god our species has ever created, 'Cash', is infinite. Its followers control governments and to maintain control they force citizens to worship. Most citizens have become meaningless pawns ruled by debt and economic servitude - their states run by pious fanatics who see them as convenient sources of revenue.

They've been made into worthless citizens, left to fend for themselves against the god kings who wage economic war on them.

It is time for atheists, for humanists, for the rational and the thoughtful and the enlightened, to take back control of the species. When our world has grown so small we can no longer hide from *one another, we should be working towards the betterment of us all.*

*There is no other answer that allows our survival.*

*Men, women and children are dying needlessly. Faced with endless human carnage, simply being an atheist is not only insufficient, it is immoral.*

*The only rational response to such insanity is anger.*

*Its only remedy, action.*

*We are told religion is required to bring morality to mankind, but the sanctified codes of these religions are all lies. Think of the Madonna and Child, perhaps the most iconic image of the Christian church next to the Crucifixion, an eternal image of beauty, torn bloody from our ancestral memory and then perverted, in order to sell us an earthbound deity who never existed.*

*And it is not the only human virtue stolen.*

*Compassion, empathy, altruism and the ability to forgive. Our noblest traits don't belong to any gods. They are ours; they belong solely to humanity, and the religions and cults who claim to possess these traits possess nothing more than degraded and abused copies.*

*It cannot be stated strongly enough: atheists must never worry about being the moral or intellectual inferior of any religious being because the atheist has the insurmountable advantage of clarity.*

*The religious mind does not observe the world; it only observes how it must be changed to suit its psychosis. Reality must be distorted before a religious follower can even begin to interpret it. The atheist understands truth can only be imagined by those who do not first shield their eyes behind their ideologies and rhetoric.*

*Ideology and rhetoric are the enemies of intelligent thought, primarily because they look so much like it. To be free of the gods is to be free to see the world. Truth is something an atheist learns, not something they teach.*

*Think of our species as we developed through time. We once lived without the gods, but that world was co-opted, erased, buried and vilified by the creators of the gods. We've forgotten the gods didn't create the garden of Eden, their earthly creators simply kicked us out.*

*In response to that violence, I reclaim, on behalf of my species, our ancestral birthright. A world free of gods.*

*A world whose ultimate measure of good and evil would be the effect of our actions on humanity. In the world of the enlightened, the evil we do becomes ours.*

*A world where the needs of a child are regarded first. Food, shelter, love, guidance. Civilization was born to protect the family in whatever form it takes, and it must return to that duty.*

*A world where each generation understands we have a duty to our descendants and the world they will inhabit. Not as the stewards of this world, but as one of its many creations.*

*A world where gender dictates nothing more than our role in the creation of new life, rather than our ability to create, or reason, to analyze or judge or work. Anything less is a betrayal against the species and we will suffer for it.*

*A world where business ideology is made to serve the public good. We must remove the corporate veil, and fiat currency must be tethered to reality once again. The choice between low cost or ethical products must become an archaic concept. Disposable products must become an anachronism.*

*I know the gods, so violently entrenched in our collective subconscious, will not allow humanity to end their reign. Not easily. I'm ready to face the gods and their followers, and I hope I am not alone. I believe our species must outgrow the mental illness we have allowed to corrupt our history, or it will end our history. The gods are killing us. The survival of our species has become a war of attrition.*

*And to those religious who feel atheists are being too aggressive towards them, think about how atheists see the world for a moment.*

*We look at humanity and see endless potentials. Endless possibilities. We are the culmination of millions of years of good luck, and our very consciousness is a gift so precious as to be difficult to put into words. The future represents to us limitless adventures, countless discoveries, entire universes to explore and understand. The amount of good in us is infinite, and all we have to do to find it is open our eyes.*

*Then we look at what we have become.*

*Ruled by men who force us to worship imaginary beings, and who will oftentimes kill us if we don't. The creativity, the potential, the greatness that is the human spirit, all of it crushed under the need of these religious fanatics to feel validated. Entire nations robbed of their humanity. Women stripped of their rights. Endless wars, killing not just soldiers, not just worshippers, but everyone, no matter their allegiance.*

*The future of our species, robbed from us for nothing more than mythologies. Ego. Endless suffering for no greater purpose than to appease a Bronze-Age intellectual band-aid.*

*In other words, if you are a follower of a god, you are not part of humanity's bright future. Your self-indulgent fantasies place you squarely in its sordid and violent past.*

*But we are thinking beings, and nothing is written in stone ...*

*It has always been our sincerest hope you could see it in yourself to join us, because in spite of our differences we are all part of the same genetic brotherhood. There is enough room in the future for everyone.*

*It is important you decide where you stand, because if our societies don't turn away from the insanities of religion, eventually the weight of humanity will fall on the shoulders of the last person standing. As realization of the truth comes to them, they will have nothing left to do but look inward to themselves to lay blame.*

*Alone in the universe. Standing alone in the desolation that was once our greatness.*

## SEPTEMBER 23, NIGHT 38

I open the book - I'm dreaming again. I'm used to this and I can spot the signs.

My vision is sharp and I can see my writing. I look at the script and it is so happy to see me, shiny and clean on official-looking paper. I wrote for two days, scratching the words onto the pages. I'm so proud of them, they make me feel bigger.

I can see the top of my wife's old car below me, driving quickly along a dark and empty highway. She is speeding past fields of grass. The life I know is there, opaque to my dreaming vision. Hellen is behind the wheel and she is talking very loudly. I want to hear her - I'm sitting in the passenger seat. I can smell rain in the air, and Hellen is mad at me.

"Do you have any idea how inappropriate it is to start preaching about helping poor people during a company dinner?" she shouts. "Nobody cares the little brown people are starving, or why the Pope should do more. Nobody cares what you think! How am I supposed to go to work in two weeks? How am I supposed to face my boss after you accuse him of being some sort of hypocritical religious fanatic?"

Her face is red, reflecting her boiling anger. She lets it flow in a torrent - her words blurring into one another.

I am silent. This is familiar and I think I know what she's going to say next.

"You think you are so above me and my friends, and yet look at you. A slob who drives a bus! A fucking bus! You think you can tell my boss he should be better? Tell me? He buys and sells bus companies for fun, people like you owe him your lives. You'll be lucky if he doesn't decide to have you fired! What has gotten into you? What is with this sudden decision to be so very atheistic? Are you trying to make enemies or something?"

Her breathing is fast, and I watch as she forms the next volley in her mind. She is not used to such angry outbursts. Hellen comes from a world where emotion is wrong. Unacceptable unless it's warm and saccharine - vanilla love on white toast in the morning. This emotional outburst, this heated display of truth, is causing her problems thinking, problems steering the car.

I remember this.

The rain is falling gently onto the windscreen and we are travelling down a highway. A familiar highway. Far off in the distance I can see a bridge spanning the road. It's so dark. The cars travelling across it are dark as well, and the lights they shine into the night face away from us, offering no illumination.

"You don't love me anymore, do you?" she asks. Her tone is quiet; she knows what my answer will be. She knows I love her ... but our worlds are too different. She will feel betrayed, as she did the first time we had this conversation, and I'm so sad our attempt to reconcile our differences has ended with such finality.

I sit silently. The wheels hum on the wet road as we travel into the night, so much night to travel through it seems. Hellen and I are looking ahead. We both feel it. The end. Nothing comes after this chapter and the book will finish without telling us the answers.

"I can't keep this up. I can't," she moans. Her hands grip the wheel hard as she tries her best to maintain the control she was taught from such an early age. "I can't."

"We don't have to," I answer. "Nobody said we had to."

"It's not that easy. What will my family say? Work? They think you're some sort of blue collar nut case, and they see me as the fool who married him," she says, pausing.

We both take a breath.

"You have to come back. We can't stay separated any longer. It's the proper thing to do," she says.

"Do you really believe that?"

She shoots a look at me; she knows where I'm taking this. She always forgets I'm no longer bound by her laws, and whenever I act immune to them it always catches her by surprise.

The night races past us and I remember looking at the speedometer. It had shocked me when I looked the last time and I look again. How did we end up going so fast?

I can feel the last words being read out loud.

The bridge is coming. It will pass over us and we will be home. The night will comfort us and our love will find a way. The car, our armour in the shining night, keeps us warm and safe. The tires hum under us on the wet road, in the wet air, and I tell Hellen she should slow down.

Hellen sets her jaw and turns the wheel. I watch her hand move the light switch to the off position. I remember how she did it. The night takes over as the car becomes dark. The hum of the wheels changes. I feel the road go soft, spongy, and the car turns. The speed. It's too much, and the darkness is complete as the bridge looks for us. The lights on the dashboard are hard to see. So much vibration. In the green light I can see Hellen's leg, her thigh, pressed hard and straight on the gas pedal. The engine loves the attention and this expensive car takes charge of our future.

The bridge is coming. Yellow crash barrels appear large behind Hellen. I remember to scream at her, just as I did before, but it's her turn to go silent. She sees my writing, the clean pages glowing in the darkness on my lap. She reaches for them and shakes them in my face. They become covered in blood and I'm horrified to see what she's done.

Satisfied, she turns her head against the violent motions of this drawn out murder, and as the last words are read from the book, she speaks:

"Fuck you."

... darkness.

I can see the car, half-crushed, resting on its roof. The only wheel still attached to the frame is immobilized, bent and alone. Our affairs have become nothing more than worthless rubble hurled randomly into the dust. Hellen's drivers licence sits in the hard stubble of grass next to the road, and the smears of blood that obscure her name are already drying. I look closer and I can't help but feel sorry for her.

I see Hellen's smiling face next to what remains visible of her name...

... Mrs. Hell ...

The book ends.

# 39

## SEPTEMBER 24, AFTERNOON

I'm going home.

Markus and Lacy visited me earlier today, and we said our goodbyes. I've invited them to visit me in a few weeks at my home, once I've had a chance to get myself organized, and they both seemed happy for the offer. Keeping in touch isn't going to be difficult as I'll be seeing Lacy a few times a week for therapy. It's going well, but I still have a lot of work to do. I feel comfortable around the two of them, and they have grown into a couple in my mind. I like that.

A funny thing. While giving Markus my number I froze, I couldn't remember it, and after a bit of thought I realized why.

I was inviting people from this world, this medical world full of the pains and terrors I've been facing, into my world. A world I haven't rebuilt yet, because from the moment Hellen turned the wheel in the dark it ceased to exist. I don't know what to expect when I arrive home. I don't even know who I'll be. Am I going to be able to speak with

Markus and Lacy in a social situation? A part of me knows we probably won't keep in touch, at least I imagine the odds are against it, and I find that thought a bit sad. What do we have in common after all, other than the common goal of getting me healed? Once that's gone, what will be left?

I'll show them my writing. Perhaps there will be something in it we can share.

The doctor was in earlier as well, and as usual I was amazed at his inability to connect with me on any level. We discussed things like my scars, my crutches, and the frequency of my home-care visits. All very practical stuff, and not once did the man ever ask me how I was doing. I find that disconcerting, the ability he has to not find me. Realistically I can't say he is a friend, but with his help I've been able to survive Hellen's spiritual crisis, and I would have thought he would feel a connection at some level for his part in that. Certainly more than the curt "good luck" and the handshake he offered me before leaving. I suppose it's just what it is - a person's way of dealing with hard emotions, so I probably shouldn't feel slighted by it. Perhaps in the weeks and months ahead my visits will reveal a different side of him, as I leave the reality of my recovery behind and assume the mantle of humanity more openly.

It's another gorgeous day, and I'm glad to be leaving during such nice weather. I've resolved to visit my old park once I'm more mobile, and as I sit here on my bed I'm reminded I haven't seen Soleil for a few days. The writing has kept my head down, my mind distracted, and I've rarely looked up to see if he was there.

My thoughts are blunted today. Muted. The day feels draped in socks and my vision sees too much future and too much past.

Today should be more of an event, but every noise, every smell, every groan and yell from the ward say this is just another day, and my departure is barely a single brushstroke on that great fresco of life. I was the purpose of bed 4b, its reason for being, and soon I'll be replaced. Another follower will take my station and they will be worshipped for their need as I was.

Too many gods in my head, fighting for life.

My legs and my arms look thin, so very thin, but the bruising is mostly gone and I'm looking more whole. My arm is stronger, and it's been amazing to see the speed of its recovery. It wasn't long ago I couldn't even hold a glass of water to my lips with that hand, and now I can write with it again. I wrote for two days, and the worst hardship I endured was cramping. If I could thank my body, I would. I can easily walk twenty feet with my crutches now. Every step was paid for in sweat and tears, but the mortgage is already paid, and now it's just practice.

The random chance of matter that is me is working as it should, and I live in this temple in awe of its skill.

My little poem, my spiritual ultimatum, is sitting on the table next to me. Lacy was nice enough to have found a brown envelope for it, but I'm afraid to show it to anyone. I'm proud of what I'm learning, proud of my new perspectives, but that first step, the one that takes all this thought from the inside to the outside ... I'm intimidated. I feel like I'm no longer walking a comfortable path anymore, and what the future brings is a mystery. I think the best way to describe me today would be an anti-theist (if such a word even exists) and that's not a safe place to be. I just want humanity to thrive and grow, and isn't that what we all want?

I don't think so. Not anymore.

There must be others that feel as I do. I know there are. Funny how alone I can feel in spite of knowing I'm not. I'll eventually find them, but until then, this illusion of solitude remains.

It's the day. This day I say goodbye. I'm melancholy, and the idea of sleeping in my own bed tonight is scary. My bed on this ward, bed 4b, is my home, and as much as I want to leave, there exists a part of me that wants to stay. Needs to stay. I don't feel ready to live again, and the idea of being alone in my home makes me tense. All of my comfortable junk, the knick-knacks and mementos that represent my time here in this life, won't be able to calm me as I make my way to this new place I am.

I'm a stranger moving into another man's home. His death was slow, but he's gone, and I'll need to deal with his things.

This mood of mine is not helping and I look out the window for what might well be the last time. The sun is high, and the few clouds that appear are mostly for effect, just a bit of a break from the broad canvas that is today's wispy-blue fall sky. In the distance people are walking, their pets along for the ride, and I pass time watching them. So often have I spent days doing this in a stupor from the drugs, from the pain, from my thoughts.

Today I'm alone. My thoughts are calmer, my pain under control, and the drugs a fading memory. The people walking are so carefree, they really are just taking a walk in the park, after all. I trace the swing of their legs in my mind, the endless pendulum of time measured in steps through a field.

They are doing the work, taking the steps, and yet it's me who sees the importance of it. Perspective really is everything in this world.

A nurse arrives with a smile and I recognize her. She tells me it's time to get dressed, and I know what's supposed to happen afterwards. I'll be taken off the list of patients, off the list of worshippers, and then I'll be ferried home. That was part of the doctor's meeting with me, and if all goes well I'll be greeted by my homecare nurse when I arrive.

I remember a story I heard as a child. The story of the River Styx, and the ferryboat carrying souls to the land of the dead. It fascinated me, but I am going to do it differently. The ferry boat pilot, Charon, is going to guide me back across the river, and the souls of the dead are to be left behind as I return to the land of the living. To a world I'll barely recognize. He'll be waiting for me at my door, and he'll show me how to live there again. He will show me how to feed my cat.

Franklin, my friend - the only survivor of my time away.

The bronze is glowing warmly in the light. The beauty of my sculpture is doing its best to show me the good in things, and I hold my breath waiting for time to pass. The taxi will be here soon, I'll be dressed, papers will be signed, and they will wheel me out the door.

I have so much work to do, and I hold the brown manila envelope that holds my future close to me.

## SEPTEMBER 24, EVENING — 40

I had forgotten I have steps to my front door. Five of them, and after doing battle with my limbs I'm finally inside my house - my tired looking home, resting on my couch.

The ride in the taxi was an experience I hadn't expected. The driver seemed prepared for everything, and each time I mentioned I needed help, he was ready. He told me they use him regularly to transport patients home, and I was surprised to hear it. What if something goes wrong? When we arrived he had my house key ready, and he brought my bag in and helped me up the steps. The hospital had arranged a few bits of gear to be left on my doorstep, and he put those inside as well. As he finished, the homecare nurse arrived.

Another big guy. Bigger than I was anyway, and we talked for a long time as he prepared my house for its new occupant. He unpacked and assembled the medical equipment, and I could see I'd been given a whole range of accessories to make my home more manageable. I'm hoping I won't need them for long, but they have already made themselves useful. We talked about how I would live, and we agreed I should stay on the main floor for a while, at least until I have enough strength to go up the stairs alone safely.

Before the accident, I frequently considered removing the shower from the main floor bathroom. I always thought it was odd having a shower on the main floor, and now it's going to be my hygienic bread and butter. My toothbrush and cloth arranged, we talked about food and sleeping arrangements.

It wasn't long before I realized nobody had told him about Franklin. A few quick calls and I had the vet's office on the line. Franklin had been staying with a foster family, and he told me they could have him back home that evening. I was glad to hear we would be together again so quickly, and was surprised such a thing as a foster family for pets even existed. The vet told me it was a volunteer program his office organized, and he was obviously proud of it. I was so impressed at the thoughtfulness, I told him I would like to offer my own home once I was feeling better, and I hung up feeling more connected to humanity than I have in months ... years.

My homecare nurse will be in twice a day. His name is Mike.

It's been such a long time since I've been in my house, and the smells are wrong. Familiar but stale. Comfortable but strange. My two tanks had been emptied by a local aquarium shop a long time ago, but the scent of empty tanks, of the dead coral rocks and the mouldering water on the bottoms of reservoirs, had left their mark. The fridge was worse, and Mike spent at least an hour disposing of food that had made biological history. He'll do some grocery shopping for me before he returns tomorrow morning, and I expect I'll be eating large. Whatever I have, I hope the smell does some good to this place.

It's quiet here.

I examine my living room. The walls are empty, the plants are dead, and the curtains are drawn. I can see my home has become a crypt and a shudder passes through me. I'm not anxious to start moving yet, but the feeling of death is too much for me and I manage to upright myself and stagger my way to the curtains. My crutches are working well on the hardwood floor, and for that small favour I'm thankful.

I part the curtains and look outside.

Fall has arrived here as well, and the few meagre trees I can see have changed. The sidewalk is not busy, but there are people walking their dogs, and the traffic is regular and loud. Much louder than I could hear in my hospital room. I feel a bit overwhelmed. I'm back in the middle of life again, and after such a long break, part of me wonders how I'll fit.

I open the curtains completely and the light accepts the invitation. The heat of the sun on my skin makes me feel good. Stories of distant worlds fill my head as the light brags of its conquests, and I enjoy my foolish thought. The room looks better in this happy light, so I tour my own home and say hello to my old things. So many sad goodbyes on the horizon, so much of my past will be gone forever, but today, tonight, my first few hours back home, we will talk and remember.

My notes from the hospital are by the couch, and I wonder about them.

What are they?

These two worlds, my past and my present, are together here, and the thoughts I'm having don't leave me any room. My past is gone, and this place makes me feel like I'm married to a stranger.

I stop. My mind slows.

When I'm better, I'll leave.

Cleanly, the decision has been made.

My body hurts quite a bit from this activity, but the need to be back is strong, and I shuffle from foot-to-foot through the main floor, opening more curtains. Letting the light in. It's late in the afternoon and it will probably be dark within a few hours, but I don't care. I want to see. The humans out there are a part of me, and I've missed them.

My sculpture and its hidden friend. Soleil. Markus and Lacy. The park. Hellen. The pain. All of it comes back to me as I settle myself onto the couch, and I let them go. So much emotion has been building towards this moment and I let it all go. The future is coming and I'm ready.

"Goodbye Hellen, I am so sorry we couldn't be better for each other." I speak the hopeful words into the room, but she's gone.

The tears are quiet. Gentle. I let them happen. I'll make it, I know I will, and this is just the last gentle wave while the ship leaves the dock.

The light begins to fade and the darkness allows my thoughts to calm. I turn on a lamp I had forgotten I owned. The incandescent light is warm on my hand, and I allow myself the pleasure. Beside the lamp sits my handwritten canon, waiting. I know I'm not finished, but I'm happy I've begun. I've never owned a computer, but I think I want one now. I want to share.

I watch as the shadows change on the unfamiliar paint, on the walls that feel wrong.

The darkness of my first day back has arrived, and I'm tired and thirsty. I make my way to the kitchen and let the water run for a while, and when I'm satisfied it's fresh, I have a drink. The cold is nice, and my stomach is anxious for something more. The cupboards are empty, so for a moment I'm resigned to waiting for Mike to bring breakfast.

Then I remember.

With effort, I manage to get a small pot to the sink, let it fill with water, and turn on the burner. My hospital bag is still in the front hallway, and I make my way there, turning lights on as I go. As I arrive, the doorbell rings informing me the family who has been watching Franklin has arrived. I'm exhausted, but this familiar humanity surrounding me, the routine of people, feels good to me. I call out for them to enter, and as I do, I take my dinner out of my bag.

A flood of new friends fills my hallway. Their voices and their children are welcomed into this temporary home I inhabit, and I feel my love return. We are a beautiful species. I can see Franklin in his carrier, and as we make our way to the kitchen to let him out, I look forward to our furry conversations.

Children talking, parents comforting, and I'm warm and safe. My hand is getting stronger, and I listen to the children telling me stories of Franklin's adventures as I pour the macaroni into the boiling water.

# EPILOGUE
## The Atheist Bible

The Atheist Bible was never intended to be any sort of final word. Others have spoken at great lengths on everything I've touched upon, and they've done so more eloquently. Find them. They have explored our humanity to depths I haven't even intimated in these pages, and if you're exploring the world of atheism or humanism for the first time, they will be the ones to take you further. My self-assigned purpose in writing The Atheist Bible was to be a gentle first step - and to remind those individuals (who might never have heard the ideas contained within these pages) that atheists, for want of a better way of phrasing it, came first.

Religions today are not belief systems, they are business models. They are a means of harvesting wealth and power; protected by violence, subterfuge, and the weight of tradition. It is my dream that one day atheists and humanists the world over will be able hold their heads up and proclaim their non-affiliation, safely and proudly. We are not there yet. The worst crimes being committed against our species and our planet are being done in the name of the gods, and at the top of the list sits that most cruel and spiteful god of all, cash. In my opinion, the greatest toll on our numbers is the body count created in search of corporate profit. I truly believe that until we end the reign of these gods, until we limit their influence and censure their grasping desire for power, our species has no hope of a future ... at least not a future I would be willing to send my children into.

## ABOUT MICHAEL LEAMY

Michael Leamy was born in Montreal, has lived all over Canada, and now lives in Victoria, British Columbia, with his wife and three children.

He can be found on Twitter @Michael_Leamy, or occasionally on his blog MICHAEL SAID ... http://www.michaelleamy.ca/

Made in the USA
Charleston, SC
03 December 2013